NO MAN RIDES ALONE

NO MAN RIDES ALONE

by

Dave Waldo

Dales Large Print Books
Long Preston, North Yorkshire,
BD23 4ND, England.

British Library Cataloguing in Publication Data.

Waldo, Dave
    No man rides alone.

    A catalogue record of this book is
    available from the British Library

    ISBN   1-84262-393-1 pbk

First published in Great Britain in 1965
by Ward Lock and Company Limited

Copyright © 1965 by Dave Waldo

Cover illustration © Faba by arrangement with
Norma Editorial S.A.

The moral right of the author has been asserted

Published in Large Print 2006 by arrangement with
Dave Waldo, care of Rupert Crew Limited

Dales Large Print is an imprint of Library Magna Books Ltd.

Printed and bound in Great Britain by
T.J. (International) Ltd., Cornwall, PL28 8RW

TO
EMMA

CHAPTER ONE

I'd run into a bit of trouble on my way north in a saloon in Julesburg with two gents who thought I was someone else and before you could say a good goddam I was hightailing it out of there with a posse on my trail. Well, that wasn't the first time and I shook 'em off in some wild country just north of the Platte and continued on my way to look for what was worth seeing in Wyoming territory. It wasn't long since Custer and his men had been trapped at the battle of the Little Big Horn and the country was still pretty wild and empty except around the few towns that had grown up near the railroad. I made a big circle west of Cheyenne where they have a lot of law, especially for those who can afford it. A couple of days' riding brought me into country that looked mighty fine. It was late afternoon and I'd come up over a sunbaked ridge. What I saw was unexpected. Pines and oak grew up out of the hillside just below where I sat on Bessie. They shaded off some hundreds of feet down into a wide basin, golden now in the late afternoon sunlight except where the surrounding hills threw shadows across the valley grass. And the basin itself ran for a long way, twenty–thirty miles I figured, up to some big mountain peaks at the far northern end.

I just sat there drinking it all in, the golden sunlight, the green valley, the distant high country shouldering up into the soft blue afternoon sky, the solitude, the peace.

'This is the place for folks like you an' me, Bessie,' I said.

Bessie twitched her left ear to show she'd heard and I just went on leaning on the saddle-horn and dreaming about having a snug couple of quarter sections somewhere in that valley and a neat little herd of cattle a-grazing on them.

Then, Crack! Wham! A gun went off and

my stetson took to the air and sailed downhill. There wasn't any more time for dreaming. I dug spurs into Bessie, pulling her head round at the same time and we shot off along the ridge back into the shelter of some pines west of where we'd been resting and under the lee of the ridge. When we were well in among the trees I pulled Bessie to a halt and climbed out of the saddle. There hadn't been much time for thinking or feeling, but now I felt pretty mad, especially without my stetson. I'd had it a long time and only took it off to go to bed. Anyways, I kind of objected to being a target for some gent with a grudge. The whole goldarned incident was too familiar. It reminded me of the past, which I figured I was riding out of, and my little dream of a happy future was all shot to pieces along with my best hat.

Well, I made sure Bessie was tied to a pine branch. Then I made my way back to the ridge and began a bit of plain and fancy scouting.

The slug that got my hat had come from

east of where I'd been admiring the view so I made my way down the southern slope of the hill and worked across to a point below where I thought the bushwhacker ought to be. Any kind of dispute, as far as I'm concerned, has got to be settled at close quarters. As you may or may not know, I'd lost the use of my right hand in a little fracas with the Owens boys at Newtown in Arizona a few months back. I'd learned to use my left hand when I'd teamed up with Dan Maffrey in New Mexico and it had had a busy time when we'd had a run-in with the Fenton gang in and around Gilburg Crossing. But that's another story. What really mattered was that I could use a Colt pretty well but rifle work was a more difficult matter so far as I was concerned.

Well, I inched my way up through bushes and small-growth pines until at last I was a long way east of where I'd originally been sitting peaceably on Bessie. There was a knob of rock ahead of me just on the spine of the ridge and I worked my way round east of it, figuring that if some mean hombre was still there he'd be keeping an eye on the western side.

And I was right. As I edged my way round the rock there he was, a small jasper with his back to me, sitting cross-legged on a ledge which looked down along the whole length of the ridge. He had a useful-looking Winchester cradled across his knees. I eased my six-gun out of the holster and spoke kind of soft, not to flurry him.

'Jest raise your hands, mister, an' grab a little air.'

I saw him go rigid with surprise so I gave him a few more instructions.

'Don't try anything fancy with that cannon on your lap. Jest stand up slow an' easy an' let it slide on to the ground. In case you've got any foolish notions, jest listen.'

And I clicked back the hammer of the Colt in my left hand. Well, that settled it. He raised his hands well above his head. Then he edged the rifle off his knees on to the ground and slowly stood up, still with his back to me. A neat, fairly small man and a bit of a dandy too judging from the tight-fitting pants he was wearing. Still these hombres are often the most dangerous.

'Right,' I said. 'Now you can turn round but do it slow an' easy.' He did as he was bid and I saw that he wasn't wearing a gun. Then I saw him and was even more surprised. Instead of a rough, sinful-looking hombre I was face to face with a handsome boy with soft blue eyes and what looked like flaxen hair showing under the brim of his stetson.

'Well,' I said, kind of stern. 'What in hell do you mean by ventilatin' my best hat an' giving me grey hairs at my time of life?'

He just stood there, saying nary a word and actually going slightly red in the face.

'There's folks I've known down the trail who'd have filled you full of lead instead of jest a-talkin' as I am,' I went on. 'What goes on around here, if a feller like me can't sit in his saddle for a breathing while and admire the scenery?'

He mumbled something under his breath

but I couldn't hear what it was. He was a mighty shy and retiring kind of hombre, especially for a gunslinger and dry-gulcher.

I said, 'I figure you owe me a debt. To put it in a word – a hat. Reckon yours ought to fit. Throw it over, mister.'

He sort of yelped out, 'No.'

I said, 'All right. Then I'll come an' get it.'

So I holstered my Colt and strode purposefully towards him. I could see panic in his soft blue eyes and then suddenly he whipped off the stetson and I stopped in my tracks, dumbfounded. It wasn't a boy at all. It was a girl whose golden hair now glistened and waved in the sunlight on the ridgetop.

'Well,' I said at last. 'If this don't beat all.'

'Now that you've satisfied your curiosity,' she said, a mite haughtily, 'perhaps you'll let me ride on my way.'

This remark, added to the shock of my first surprise, left me with my mouth open like a fish out of water. But I recovered and spoke again with some sternness; not an easy matter when you're talking to a beautiful young girl.

'There's jest two things wrong with what you've said, ma'am. First I ain't curious. Second it was you who tried to stop me riding on my way with a slug from that Winchester of yours.'

'Yes,' she sort of sighed. 'I was just hoping I could get away with it.'

'A slug from a rifle takes a lot of getting away from,' I said, sociably. I was beginning to feel a certain pleasure in her company. There are worse ways of spending a nice summer afternoon. 'I'd still like to know why you put a slug through my best hat.'

She just stood there a while saying nothing. Then at last she seemed to make up her mind.

'I'm beginning to think that perhaps after all you're a genuine stranger and not another of the dry-gulching scoundrels driftin' into the Basin and stirring up trouble.'

'Ma'am,' I said. 'I've been side-steppin' trouble for as long as I can remember. I was

16

jest a-ridin' thru' and then you came after me with that gun of yours.'

'There's a gang of rustlers operating in the hills around the valley,' she said in her direct crisp sort of way. 'Some of 'em make out that they're small ranchers and now they're banding together against my Pa and his friends. Lately they've begun bringing in gunslingers from all over. We're aiming to discourage 'em, which is why I put a bullet through your hat.'

'You've kind of reached the point of firin' first and askin' questions afterwards?' I said, with growing respect.

'That's about it,' she said. 'And now if I were you I'd ride on a couple of hundred miles or so until you're well out of range and as fast as that old jughead of yours will carry you.'

Now I can take a lot of hard words about myself but when folks start calling Bessie rude names like 'jughead' and such I get kind of riled so when I spoke I sounded a bit dry even to myself.

'That hoss of mine ain't old, miss, and I sure take exception to the word "jughead".' I gave her a pretty fierce look. 'Above all I don't take kindly to threats or advice.'

'Have it your own way, stranger,' she said more than a mite proudly. 'I was trying to do you a favour. This Basin's a powder-keg and if you're not careful you'll find yourself sitting on the lid when she blows up.' She paused and gave me a look as chilly as a January wind in the high Sierras. 'With your kind permission I'll now be on my way home.'

'Where's home?' I said.

'Ask anyone you see in this valley where the Urquharts are and they'll tell you, stranger. I am Sarah Urquhart.' She said it just like 'I am Queen Victoria.'

'Thank you,' I said. 'You may go.'

That really burned her up but she held back the words and walked away towards a clump of pines just east of where we'd been having our little chat. I waited and after a bit I heard a horse move away into a trot and then go tearing away downhill.

Well there wasn't much more for me to do up on that ridge so I decided to try and find my stetson. I went back to where I'd originally halted and looked around but there wasn't any trace of the hat anywhere. I poked around for a good fifteen minutes but in vain. My much prized J.B had vanished. I went back to where I'd left Bessie. Being without a hat is, next to being without a gun, like being naked. There was only one thing to do and that was to ride down to the nearest township and buy another hat, so I climbed on to Bessie and we ambled off eastwards and then downgrade more or less in the direction taken by my dry-gulching lady-friend.

We followed a trail that led right down the ridge slope through pines and oak. It swung east after a time and levelled out. We came out of the timber at last and then, not more than half a mile away, was a small town. As I rode nearer I could see it was a quiet sort of place with a wide main street running between two long rows of buildings with a few shacks spreading out at the rear of each row. Just the kind of settlement you find anywhere in the West. I rode on in.

The first houses I passed were dwellings – a bit quiet and closed-up-looking but in pretty good shape with fence-rails and white painted porches. The kind of place a man could sit on and have a bit of peace. There were some stores after the houses. Dry goods, a gun-shop, another dry goods, a livery stable, Abraham's Emporium, a barber-shop, a saloon – The Cattleman's House, a photographer's studio, a saloon called The Trail. I gave it a careful look. Saloons are mighty fine places but you have to be careful about which one you go into.

There was a tie-rail outside the next saloon – The North Platte. I angled over to it, climbed out of the saddle and flung Bessie's reins around the rail. The saloon was pretty large with a big false front of weathered boards and the name in fancy script across the width of it. It had bat-wing doors at the entrance. I climbed on to the sidewalk and pushed them inwards with a practised hand.

Maybe I've had too much practice. Maybe I never learn from experience. Maybe I should've remembered The Golden Nugget and the Owens boys back in Newtown or Mitch Fenton and Dan Maffrey in The Bonanza at Gilburg Crossing. But just then I didn't remember any of these things. All I knew was that I hadn't eaten for a good many hours and that my throat and mouth were as dry as the Arizona desert.

There was a long bar down the left side of the room and some hombres sitting at a table at the back. A couple more were propping up the bar behind which a fat man with a curled moustache was pouring something into a glass. As I stood in the entrance whatever talk was going on died away and when I walked across to the bar it was in a silence so loud that I could hear the watch in my vest pocket ticking. I got to the bar, choosing a spot so that the two men were between me and the other group at the table.

The barman looked at me and said, 'What can I do for you?'

Now this seemed to me a mite peculiar.

'Well,' I said, 'there's one thing you can't do, bartender, and that is do my drinking for me.'

That one sank well in. The silence boomed away around us and the barman's face changed colour – medium red to dark red.

Before he could say any more, I said, 'I'll have whisky. The kind you keep for your friends.'

He hesitated a moment and looked across at the group around the table but no one said anything and he reached for a bottle and shot-glass. It was just about as cosy as a rattlesnake's den. He pushed the bottle at me and I filled myself a snort. It was out of the right bottle and I poured myself another. I drank the second one slowly and between sips I rolled myself a cigarette and admired the bar-furnishings. For a small town in the middle of the Wyoming desert they were pretty fancy. A solid mahogany bar and back of it a long gilt-edged mirror which gave me a good view of the room behind me. Above the mirror there was a big oil-painting of some deer with mountains behind them. There were a pair of silver spurs hanging from a nail on the wall. The bartender stood and watched me as my eyes roved round.

'Everything to your taste, mister?' There was a sort of edge to the question that I didn't really like but I replied mildly.

'It's all mighty fine. Who paid for it all, I wonder?'

'What's that to you?' said a voice behind me. I looked in the mirror. One of the men who'd been sitting at the table when I came in had snuck up on me.

'You shouldn't do things like that,' I said, turning slow and careful and getting myself a good look at the man as I did so. At first I just had an impression of a pint-sized hombre with very white hair and pale blue eyes – an old-timer full of small curiosities. Then I had a second look and saw that the eyes were the kind of blue you see in thick winter ice, the skin of his face was like saddle leather, lined with wear but not with

23

age and that he wore a gun low-down. It looked as if it had been used – a lot.

'And why shouldn't I do things like that?' he was saying. It was just a question asked in a gentle sort of way. But with something underneath the gentleness that I didn't understand – not just then.

'I knew a gent once,' I said, 'that did just what you did.'

'And what was it he did?' Just a quiet prompting sort of question.

'He snuck up on another gent just like you snuck up on me.' I paused but he didn't say anything, just stood there, sort of idly curious.

'It was kind of unfortunate,' I continued, looking him smack in his cold blue eyes. 'My friend had itchy fingers and when the gent spoke suddenly my friend just spun round and blew a hole through him.'

'Like this,' said the small man softly and drew his gun so fast that I only knew he'd drawn when I saw the gun in his hand pointing straight at me. I dropped the butt of my cigarette on the bar-room floor. I only moved my fingers an inch or so to do this. Sudden movements seemed unsuitable just then.

'Now don't you get any false notions about me, mister,' I said. 'My fingers are steady-like an' I don't go round blowing holes through folks.'

'What do you go around doing, stranger?' We had come to the inevitable question at last.

'Well now,' I said. 'I figure that would be my business.'

'Let's talk about it, stranger.' The small white-haired man spun the Colt around on the trigger-guard. I watched him for a moment or so, always interested to see someone perform the road-agent's spin.

'Reckon you could call me a wayfaring man,' I said at last. 'Me and Bessie, we just ride around and take the air.'

'Where you from?' The question was no longer idly spoken.

'Way down the trail,' I said, beginning to

feel a mite irritated now.

'There's nothing for you here, stranger. The Basin's closed to you an' all your kind. Just get on that hoss of yours an' ride on. Anywhere. North, South, East or West, but don't hang around here.'

'There's a sizeable piece of Government land around here,' I said. 'Also a few acres here an' there that belong to other folks. There's nothing to stop me riding around on land that don't belong to you.'

I could see from his eyes that we'd reached a dead stop. It was beginning to look as if we could only settle our problem in one way – by gunsmoke. And then came an interruption. The doors of the saloon opened with a bang and two–three men in range clothes pushed in. Between them they half-carried, half-dragged, a wildly-struggling figure. They heaved him across the floor and finally flung him down at the white-haired man's feet. They stood away panting and getting their breath back for a bit. Then the one nearest me, a tall, broad-shouldered ranny with a two-day growth of beard said:

'We found him over in Bow Canyon, Mr Antrim. He was driving off six of our steers. He's one of the Cartledge bunch.'

Antrim, as he had been called, had turned away from me when his men came bursting in. He'd also holstered his gun. The figure, half-crouching on the floor, not much more than a boy, hatless, his black hair dishevelled, stared up at Antrim.

'I wasn't,' he shouted. 'It's a goddam lie. The critters are my Pa's.'

'And what would they be doing over in Bow Canyon?' Antrim's question was soft, deceptive.

'I sure dunno,' said the boy. 'But I found 'em there an' they're ours.'

'Nothing in the Basin's yours,' said Antrim, flatly. He paused and looked at the big unshaven hombre who'd first spoken.

'Take him outside, Enders, and teach him a lesson. A lesson he won't forget.'

I saw the boy's eyes widen with fear and I figured he knew, like a lot of other folks in

27

this neck of the woods, just what a lesson from Antrim's men would be like.

'No,' he yelled. 'No.'

They started then to drag him by the wrists across the floor. I know it was none of my business but then I'm just a mite headstrong and given to acting on the spur of the moment so I just pulled my Colt and fired once into the ceiling. All activity ceased. Antrim remained turned away from me still but no longer easy and relaxed. Just a mite rigid and almost up on the toes of his small boots.

'Back up,' I said and the three hombres who had been busy pulling the kid's wrists almost out of their sockets did as they were bid.

'Come over here,' I said to the kid and he came, eagerly. As he did so Antrim began to turn slowly, his hands well away from his sides.

'This isn't...' he began.

'I know. I know,' I said a mite impatiently. 'This isn't any of my business. Folks are always telling me that and one day I reckon I'll probably agree. As of now I'm making it my business. You've got no call to rough-up a kid for doing something you've no proof of. You ought to be ashamed. Four grown men to one undersized youngster.'

Antrim stared at me out of his cold blue eyes. They glittered with rage and watching him I was glad I had the drop on him.

'I'll kill you for this,' he managed to say at last, still quietly, and then came another interruption.

'Maybe,' said a voice, 'there's been enough killing for the time being, Jess.'

I looked across to the swing doors of the saloon and saw a big man leaning quietly against the wall. He detached himself from it as I watched and came leisurely towards us.

'Rustlin' can't be forgiven,' said the man called Jess Antrim. 'What we do with our rustlers ain't none of this stranger's business, Mr Urquhart.'

This was mighty interesting to me. This

was the big auger himself. Father of the girl who'd shot my hat off and owner of the vast acres of the Basin.

'Both your statements are true, Jess,' said the big man equably. 'But seeing as the stranger's got the drop on all of you, there isn't much you can do about it.' He looked at me. His eyes were steady and hard. He was as tough a man in his own way as Jess Antrim.

'My ramrod's right,' he said. 'But there's no need for bloodshed. You and the kid are free to go. I suggest that you keep away from the Basin in future. My hands are on the whole a little less patient than I am.'

'Folks say this is a free country,' I said. 'I ride where I like.'

He stared at me for a time, not, I reckon because he was at any loss for words but because that was his way of getting to know me.

'Who are you, stranger?'

'My name's Ross,' I said. 'Johnny Ross.'

'I'm Ed Urquhart,' he said. 'Most folks

around here know me. They'll tell you I'm always as good as my word.'

'And what's your word this time, Mr Urquhart?'

'Just ride away, Mr Ross, and there'll be no more trouble.'

I gave him a long careful look and then I said, 'Maybe. Maybe. Meantime, before I ride on there's a small matter of a stetson I've got to put right. Your daughter shot it off my head and it got lost.'

For the first time since he'd come in he looked flummoxed.

'My daughter?'

'Yessir, Mr Urquhart, your daughter. I met her up on the hill country north of here this afternoon. I figure she's got the same kind of idea about the Basin as you have.'

For a moment he just stared and then suddenly he let out a roar of laughter.

'Well, if this don't beat all.'

I waited until he'd really enjoyed the joke.

Finally he said, 'You sure have had a queer sort of welcome, Mr Ross. I guess it's up to me to make amends. If you're looking for a job I can give you one.'

'What kind of a job?'

'Why,' he said, 'herding cows, riding lines, digging post-holes. There's a lot of jobs to be done on a spread as big as mine.'

'I'll give it a thought,' I said. 'Maybe tomorrow wouldn't be too late for an answer?'

'Tomorrow will do,' he said.

The other folks in the saloon seemed less enthusiastic about me than Urquhart.

'Reckon I'll go and get myself a new hat,' I said.

'You do that, Mr Ross,' he said, and laughed again. 'Tell old Abraham to charge it up to me.'

'Thanks,' I said, and then I looked at the young feller I'd rescued from Enders and Antrim. 'You comin' my way, son?'

'Yessir,' he said, and together we made our way out of The North Platte saloon, leaving a very silent room behind us.

CHAPTER TWO

Outside I made my way to Abraham's Emporium where I hoped to get a hat. The boy paced along beside me. He was a lanky eighteen-year-old I reckoned and not the talkative kind. We reached the Emporium and I bought myself a hat fairly high in the crown and with a good wide brim to keep the sun out of my eyes. The boy stood and watched the whole transaction.

'Don't often see you hillfolks in Pitchfork,' said the storekeeper, giving him a look from under shaggy eyebrows.

'Don't often come as we ain't welcome here,' said the boy. 'This town belongs to Urquhart.'

'That ain't strictly true,' said the store-keeper. 'He owns North Platte saloon an' some houses but it's a free town to anyone

33

who chooses to ride in.'

'As long as they ride out again pretty quick,' I said.

'Mebbe so,' he said. 'But it could be better than that.' He was an old man grown careful with the years.

I pocketed the change he'd handed me and said, '*Adiós.*'

He said 'Good-day' gravely and watched us out of his shop. On the boardwalk I hesitated.

The boy said, 'You thinkin' of taking Urquhart up on his offer?'

'Maybe,' I said. 'A man's got to eat.'

'Eatin's better up in the hills,' he said. 'Maybe my Pa could use you.'

'Let's go see,' I said.

We went back to where I left Bessie. There were four other ponies racked there, three with a Circle U brand on their haunches and one unbranded chestnut. The boy went to it and mounted. I climbed on to Bessie and we rode out of town.

When we'd gone a mile or two north of the

town the boy swung his horse's head west. There wasn't much light left by this time but by what little there was I could make out a rough trail going upgrade now. It continued upgrade for another mile or two and then levelled out on to benchland. As we rode I found out that the boy's name was Dan.

'My Pa always calls me Daniel,' he said. 'But most folks seem to find Dan enough.'

He asked me where I was from.

'A long ways south of here,' I said. 'I was raised in South Carolina, fought the Yankees for three years, punched cattle in Texas. I've been around the south-west and now I'm taking a look at the north.'

'It's fine country,' he said, seriously. 'Some of the best cattle-raisin' country anywhere, my Pa says.'

'Your Pa raisin' cattle?'

'Yes,' he said. 'When the Urquharts'll let him. They claim the Basin belongs to them an' the Basin's got the sweetest grass an' most of the water. If we take cattle down

35

there they run 'em off or shoot 'em.'

'Your father buckin' this alone?'

'There's three other families along the river,' he said. 'The Brills, the Rodgers and the Smiths. There's other families farther north. Old Man Rodgers is set on movin' out. Says he's had enough. The Smiths will pull out too, I reckon. Us and the Brills won't last long agin the Urquharts. They've got the money an' the men.'

It was an old story to me. The fight for land. The fight to survive. Big man and little man. It was part of the story of Texas, of Arizona, of New Mexico. The little men called themselves homesteaders as they had the right to do by the Homestead Act. They weren't really homesteaders because they often paid for the land at a dollar twenty-five an acre after March 1877 and irrigation had to be carried out within three years of filing. The big man who had usually come first called the homesteaders a lot of things but rustler was his favourite word. Maybe at times they were. The big man had thousands of head of cattle. It didn't seem much of a crime to the little man to cut out a fat young steer some dark night, skin it down and divide it up for food. The big man thought different. These little men were criminals, outlaws. There wasn't much law in evidence in those days so you made your own. A few hands, a rope, a tree. The little man paid for his crime with his life. Plumb expensive way of eating.

'We're there now, Mr Ross,' said the boy, rousing me from my thoughts. I looked around a bit more attentively. It was full dark now but I could just make out the shape of a house. A dog barked and a door opened throwing a patch of yellow light out into the darkness. I could see the figure of a woman holding what looked like a rifle. She called out.

'That you, son?' It was a high, wary, anxious voice. It had called into the dangerous unknown before.

'Yes, Ma,' said Dan Cartledge. 'It's me. I've brung someone along of me.'

We climbed out of our saddles.

'Come on in,' said the woman. She leaned the rifle against the doorpost. The boy tied the horses to a fence. We went into the house.

'This is Johnny Ross, Ma,' said Dan. 'He saved me from a beatin'.'

'A beatin'?' The woman's voice contained no surprise. She was beyond that. But she still had fear.

'It was Matt Enders, Ma. He an' his crew caught me over on the east side with some of our strays. They took me into Pitchfork and Jess Antrim said to teach me a lesson. Reckon I know what that meant. But Mr Ross here told 'em to leave me be.'

I was looking at Mrs Cartledge as the boy's excited voice rose and fell. A typical pioneer woman. Well, maybe. She had on a long, full, greyish sort of dress and an apron tied round it. Her hair was done up in a knot on her head. Her face was young-old, tired but with something unyielding about it. Maybe ten or twenty years ago she'd been a handsome girl with fine blue eyes and hair like corn. Now the eyes were faded and her hair was turning grey.

She turned her full attention to me. 'We're sure beholden to you, Mr Ross. There's not a many round here who'll stand up to the Basin people. They've had things their own way for a long time now.'

She was looking at me with wary eyes as she talked. I saw them looking at my gun. Homesteaders don't pack guns low down or for that matter any other way. She couldn't take her eyes off it. I was the kind she was scared of. The man whose only law was that of the gun.

'Sit down,' she said at last. 'We're not over-used to having visitors but you're welcome to what we've got, Mr Ross.'

I sat on a hard chair near the fireplace.

'My husband'll be here soon,' she said. 'We eat when he comes home.'

'I'm in no hurry, ma'am,' I said. She excused herself and went off through a small door leading I guessed to a kitchen.

Dan Cartledge stood on the other side of the fireplace, watching me.

'You and your folks been here long?' It was just a question, something to break the silence with.

'Two years,' said Dan Cartledge.

'Urquharts here before you, I guess.'

'That's so,' he said. 'Mr Urquhart settled here after the war so I reckon he's been here a pretty long time.' He paused and then said hurriedly, 'That don't give him the right to think everything belongs to him or that daughter of hisn.'

'Daughter?'

'Yup,' said Dan Cartledge. 'Got some fancy name from Scotland – Sarah – an' sure thinks she's the lady of the land around here.'

I didn't say any more but the name stuck with me and I played with it for a bit in my thoughts – Sarah – Sarah. From Scotland the boy had said. I remembered what we'd heard at school about the Scots and the long wars they'd fought with the English. Tough hombres those Highlanders, even though they wore skirts, which had always struck me as plumb strange.

'She's a...' began the boy but I never learnt what he thought she was for at that moment there was the sound of riders coming into the yard and voices carrying through the still night air.

I don't know what I expected to see when the door opened but I was surprised by what I saw. The first in was a tall, raw-boned man with hard eyes and a heavy beard.

He stopped just across the threshold and stared at me.

'Who is the stranger sittin' by my hearth?' The question was addressed to no one in particular but Dan answered it.

'It's Johnny Ross, Pa. He saved me from bein' beat by the Urquhart riders.'

'I'm Ephraim Cartledge,' said Dan's Pa. 'I'm obligated to you, Mr Ross.'

He advanced towards me and held out a big hand. I took it and was sorry at once. It was like being grabbed by a grizzly bear. 'We suffer here from bad neighbours. Still the

Lord is with us.'

Other men had followed him into the room which suddenly seemed overcrowded.

'These are neighbours and friends of ours,' said Cartledge. I shook hands with them and said 'Howdy'. One was Joshua Brill whom Dan had mentioned as a neighbouring homesteader. He was the same breed as Cartledge – big and slow and kind of pious. But the other three who followed them into the room were something else, something I couldn't be wrong about. I'd ridden with their kind too long to be mistaken about them.

'This is Sam Point,' said Cartledge, indicating the man who'd come in behind Brill. 'And over by the door stand Jake Gillams and Al Rachell. Come on in and let us get this business settled, gentlemen.'

The word 'gentlemen' tickled my fancy. They all looked in my direction. Sam Point nodded, Jake Gillams said 'Howdy' in a low, harsh whisper and Al Rachell just gave me a long hard stare. I'd certainly met their kind before in the Big Bend country and up around Santa Fé. They were the scum that rises to the top after the boiling up of a war. Plenty of them had moved west after Lee's surrender in '65 and they adorned the frontier towns of every territory west of the Big Muddy. That is those that weren't planted in boothills or in narrow graves on the lone prairies. Strong-arm men for saloon-keepers, for sporting house madams and gamblers. Some got run out of town by the 'better' element and took to the back-trails and the high country and earned a dis-honest penny by road-agenting and rustling. I knew their kind and I figure from the way they gave me the eye that they knew me. We wore the mark of the outlaw. Not a matter of clothes nor even of the way a man wore a gun. It was in the eyes. Not furtive but ready. Ready for the sudden opening of a door, the hard beat of horses' hoofs, the swift movement of betrayal.

'Where you from, mister?' Jake Gillams's question came out in the same harsh whisper as his original greeting.

'Here an' there,' I said, politely. 'Mostly there.'

My answer seemed to annoy him for his face froze hard.

'You'd better start gittin' back there fast,' he said.

'Now hold hard there, Jake,' interposed Cartledge. 'We owe a debt to this gentleman if he saved my son from harm. And what's more, we could perhaps persuade Mr Ross to lend us a helping hand in our distress.'

'Yeah, sure,' I said. 'But you'll have to tell me something about this distress.'

Cartledge nodded his bear-like head sagely. 'Certainly. Certainly. That is indeed why we are assembled here tonight.' He paused for a moment and then carried straight on.

'It's an old and well-known story, Mr Ross. Good and evil in conflict. The good man at the mercy of the bad. An ancient trouble with which we are all familiar. I brought my family with God's help a thousand miles across the deserts and the prairies to this place. Our only aim was to find a home and be a trouble to none. We came through the Basin and were told to ride on by the hirelings of the man who said the Basin was his. I have never taken kindly to threats or warnings but I was resolved to cause no trouble, so we built this homestead in the hills looking out over the valley. But even this wasn't good enough for the Urquharts. They couldn't tolerate us even up in the hills and they've done everything they could to make our lives a misery. They've stolen our cattle, shot at us, torn down our fences.'

'What reason do they give?' I asked.

'None,' said Cartledge. 'Might is right for the Urquharts. They are proud and wicked people and the Good Lord will undoubtedly and in His own good time punish them for their sins. Meanwhile we, the poor home-steaders, have banded together to defend ourselves. And maybe teach the enemies of the Lord a lesson.'

'That's right,' said Sam Point, speaking for the first time.

'You got a homestead hereabouts, Mr Point?' I asked.

He favoured me with a long, searching look.

'Yes,' he said, when he'd done looking. 'These gents and me we've got a quarter-section each up around Bear Crick. We run cattle on 'em.'

'Whose?' I asked it deliberately.

Once more the long, searching examination and then a short, hard bark of a laugh and he threw the ball back at me.

'Whose do you think, mister?'

I knew what I thought and was playing with a reply when Cartledge intervened.

'Time we got down to business, gentlemen. We came here to discuss how to deal with the Urquharts – once and for all time. I suggest we talk about it.' He looked at me then. 'Are you in on this with us, Mr Ross, or are you just riding on?'

'It kind of depends on what *this* is,' I said.

'We're going to drive them out,' he said. 'Smite them hip and thigh. Only in that way will the Basin be fit for decent folk to live in.'

'Sounds like a tall order,' I said. 'From what I hear Urquhart has a big spread and enough hands to run it. Maybe twenty–thirty?'

'You leave that to us, Mr Cartledge,' said Sam Point. 'We know where we can get enough men to deal with the Urquhart crew.'

'What kind of men?' I threw the blunt question straight at him.

'That's our affair, stranger,' said Point. 'We'll do our own recruiting.' He and his two partners were watching me now with the same look as men usually give to a Gila monster. But Cartledge had to be warned before he got himself into a mess up to his middle.

'Listen, Mr Cartledge,' I said, and moved as I spoke so that I had my back to the wall. 'I figure you're going into this with your eyes shut. These men who're offering to side you are in this only for what they can get. They're not homesteaders, no more than I am. They're out to stir up the dust and if they do succeed in driving out the Urquharts, then they'll turn on you and drive you out too. There's fine fat pickings hereabouts for hombres like these.'

There was a thumping silence after these few well- or ill-chosen words and then I saw Al Rachell, who was nearest to the door, reaching quiet-like for his gun, so I beat him to it with my left-handed draw that I learned when my right hand got busted down in Arizona territory. The room seemed pretty full by now, as Ma Cartledge had joined Pa. I heard her give a quick short cry of fear but I kept my eye on Sam Point and his two friends.

'All right,' I said. 'I figure I'm odd man out here, so I'll mosey on. But remember what I've said, Mr Cartledge. Give these men one inch and they'll steal a yard. They'll start a range war hereabouts for the sheer hell of it, and everything you've built up will just burn up and blow away.'

Cartledge was silent for a while.

Then he said slowly, 'If everything the

Urquharts have built up is burned up and blown away too, then I shall be content.'

They were the words of a fanatic, as my Ma used to call the travelling preachers, and there's no arguing with such folks.

'Have it your way, Mr Cartledge,' I said. And I began to move sideways round my part of the room for the door. 'Maybe you'll remember one day I warned you.'

'He's right, dad,' I heard a voice say but I kept my eyes on Point and his pals until I reached the door. Rachell was standing near it. I raised the barrel of my gun a mite. 'Back up, mister,' I said, and he did so with as ugly a look on his misshapen face as it's ever been my bad luck to see. I opened the door with my right hand, keeping my gun steady on Sam Point with my left. Then I slid out, stepping well out of range of anyone who fired through the door after me and pulling the door to.

It was plenty dark outside but I knew where Bessie was and I cat-footed my way towards her, ready for anything to boil up in the house behind me. But nothing did. I reached Bessie and flipped the reins off the fence. She whickered softly and I led her away from the house and climbed slowly into the saddle. I'd half expected trouble but clearly they'd decided on frying more important fish. I rode away into the darkness, not too certain of the trail back to Pitchfork but luck was with me and an hour or so later I was there.

The main street wasn't big, just a scattering of stores and three saloons I'd already marked for reference. It had been a long day and I was bone-tired. I'd also been without grub for a mighty long time. I figured there'd be grub and a bed at The Cattleman's House and so I rode to the livery stable.

The liveryman was sitting just inside the door.

I climbed down.

He said, 'Howdy.'

I said the same and then asked him if he had room for Bessie.

'Room!' He gave a short sneering laugh.

'There's always room hyar, stranger.'

'So,' I said.

'Folks don't ride into Town as much as they useter. Reckon they're a spot worrit about who the'll meet. So they stay away except for buyin' grub an' grain. Then they hightail out of hyar jest about as fast as their ponies'll go.'

'Well,' I said. 'Here's one customer for you. I'll be at The Cattleman's House for the night.'

He stared at me for longer than is customary, then said, 'You'll be the feller that bucked Jess Antrim over to The North Platte.'

'Could be,' I said.

'Waal now, if this don't beat all. I'd sure like to shake your hand, stranger. You're the first feller with spunk enough to face up to Jess Antrim for I dunno how many years. We've all been waiting for this. You go on up to The Cattleman's House, stranger. You'll sure get a good welcome there.'

I was a bit puzzled by all this but I said

51

''Night' politely and walked off with my saddle bag towards the hotel. It was getting kind of late and I was hungry and tired. I wasn't quite sure that I wanted to be welcomed by anyone. I got inside the front door of The Cattleman's House and found myself in the kind of big bar-room all saloons and hotels have. It's always there with the same old smell of whisky to keep you from bed. There was a scattering of folk in it. Not the kind I'd seen in The North Platte. These were a different stripe. Townsfolk, I figured, from their clothes. In here for a drink and a small pow-wow after the day's work was done.

I went over to a solitary table not far from the end of the long bar. I sat down, aware that the talk had died on the air soon after I'd come in. I could feel their eyes on me but I was too tired to care one way or another. I wanted a drink and some chuck and some bed pretty soon.

A bartender approached. He stood idly near my chair and flapped a long white serviette.

'If you flap that thing long enough,' I said, 'you'll get up a wind that'll blow you away.'

'I was just waitin' patient-like for you to make up your mind,' he said. 'No offence intended.'

'The same goes for me, mister,' I said. 'I guess I was kind of tired an' forgot my manners. I'd like a couple of whiskies followed by a nice big steak and fried potatoes.'

'Right,' said the bartender and marched off. I sat there and he returned with a whisky bottle and a shot-glass.

'Help yourself, stranger,' he said, hospitably, and I sat watching his retreating back and then for a good half-minute after he'd disappeared through a door behind the bar. Then I turned to the bottle and poured myself a snort. I downed it in one and was about to pour a second when I was aware that folk were approaching my table.

I looked up and recognised one of them. It was Abraham from The Emporium where I'd bought my hat.

He said 'Good evening,' and when I

nodded to him, he asked, 'May we sit down with you?'

Now this surprised me a mite but without being plumb rude I had no alternative but to say, 'Help yourselves. This saloon's free for all.' While they rustled up more chairs I helped myself to my second drink and began to roll a cigarette. There were six of them. All well-dressed, well-fed, prosperous-looking, except around the eyes. These looked like the eyes of poor, uncertain men. They were anxious, shifty, troubled.

'You're Mr John Ross,' said Abraham, who seemed to have appointed himself spokesman.

'Johnny Ross to most folks,' I said. 'What of it?'

'I'm David Abraham,' he said. 'I keep The Emporium. These other gentlemen are all friends of mine. That's Ed Morgan on the left. He keeps the feed and grain store. Joe Humphress, next to him, owns the dry goods and Mike Channing runs the one and only butcher-shop in Pitchfork. Tom Roselaw owns this saloon and Gabbit the livery stable.'

I said, 'Howdy,' or nodded as each name was mentioned. Then the bartender came back with a tray and a big plate of steak and potatoes.

'You jest eat your dinner, Mr Ross. We'll do the talking,' said Abraham. He must have seen some reflection on my face of a kind of peevishness I felt at being interrupted at dinner.

I cut myself a piece of steak and began to eat.

'It's like this, Mr Ross,' began Abraham. 'Pitchfork's a place without any law. It grew up around a crossroads store that old man Benton set up for the emigrant trail and the folks moving west. Before the Indians killed him in '68 he had got himself well settled and in '69 more folks came and stayed. Ed Urquhart brought cattle up from the south. He built himself a spread and needed supplies. We brought 'em in along the overland trail. Things began to seem prosperous and peaceful. Then two years back homesteaders moved in, into the hills west of the Basin.'

'The Cartledge family, I said, chewing vigorously. I had to. The beef was tough.

'Yes. The Cartledges and others. The Urquharts didn't want 'em. They said so. But old Ep Cartledge's a stubborn man.'

'Yup. Stubborn as a mule,' put in one of Abraham's friends.

'He dug himself in and made friends with others north of the Basin.'

'The Urquharts is beginnin' to feel mighty crowded,' said Abraham's friend again.

'There's been a lot of trouble,' continued Abraham. 'Folks shot at. Cattle run off. Fences pulled down.'

'It all began after the Cartledges came,' said the liveryman Gabbit.

'Yes,' said Abraham. 'But you can't attach all the blame to the Cartledges. Ed Urquhart's a mighty hot-tempered man.'

I finished the last of my steak. It was from a tired old long-horn, I figured. He'd been far too long on the trail, like me.

56

'Why're you telling me all this?' I asked.

There was a short, heavy silence. Then Abraham spoke again.

'We figured there's only one answer to our difficulties,' he said.

'What's that?'

'You,' he said.

I was struggling with some mixed-up feelings and just about to say 'No' when the silence in the room was broken by a sudden clatter of horses outside. Riders in a hurry. Then a short burst of firing – the flat detonations of a Colt .45 and then something heavy crashed down on the boardwalk outside the saloon's front entrance.

CHAPTER THREE

The little group standing or sitting near me seemed plumb paralysed with fear. Their eyes stared and their faces whitened. I got up, loosening my gun in its holster. I walked round them towards the swinging doors at the entrance, pushing my way through a thick mist of silence. I drew my gun and eased out through the doors, ready for trouble. But everything was dead quiet, with a big, bright, silver dollar of a moon shining down and the shadows of the houses across the street black. The only thing that moved was lying just off the boardwalk. It looked like the body of a man and it raised an arm and then let it fall limp and outstretched in the dust.

I went down to where he lay and when I saw who it was I wished I'd ridden straight on and out of Pitchfork. It was Ed Urquhart lying there and he looked dead. I took a quick look up and down the moonlit street but no one showed, no one was curious. I knelt down and felt for his heart. There was no beat, no movement. Ed Urquhart was dead all right.

There were the noises of footsteps on the boardwalk. The chief citizens of Pitchfork had summoned up enough courage to come out. I half-turned towards them.

'This'll give you something to think about,' I said.

'Who is it?' Abraham's voice was a whisper laden with fear.

'It's Ed Urquhart,' I said. 'He's dead.'

One of them said, 'My God.' Then they came down and I stood aside while they picked him up and carried him to The Cattleman's House. I followed them, dragged along by something stronger than my desire to be shot of the whole thing, something I couldn't put into words, and can't now.

They took him into a small parlour off the

main bar-room. David Abraham was taking a closer look at the dead rancher. He straightened up then, slowly.

'He's been shot twice,' he said.

'Who'd have done it?' The question came from Ed Morgan.

'You know the answer to that as well as we do,' said Gabbit, the liveryman.

'Yeah. We all know the answer,' said Abraham gloomily. 'The hillfolk have taken the law into their own hands.'

'That ain't law,' said Ed Morgan fiercely. 'There ain't any law in this neck of the woods. It's every man for himself here like in the desert or the forest.'

'That's why we met here, Ed Morgan,' said Abraham. 'And you know what decision we came to.'

Ed Morgan suddenly turned his eyes on me. He was a small, dark, angry-looking hombre but he had honest eyes.

'Yes,' he replied. 'I know, but I figure we're too late.'

Abraham stared at him for a moment,

then turned his eyes towards me.

'It's like this, Mr Ross,' he said. 'Things have gone too far as you can see. That's why I said you were the answer to our difficulties when we were sitting in there.'

'I don't follow you, mister,' I said. 'I've never been an answer to anyone's problems. I'm just a fiddle-footed man who likes to ride alone and I don't want to be mixed up in anyone else's troubles.'

'No man rides alone,' Abraham said. 'Anyways, not in the Basin.'

'So,' I said dubiously.

'You come in with us, Mr Ross, if you aim to see law an' order in these parts.'

'Yes,' I said. 'I see what you mean, Mr Abraham. And just how soon do I come in with you?'

'It's quite simple,' burst in Ed Morgan. 'We want law an' order. That means we gotta have a peace-officer in this town to protect the townsfolk an' stop all this feudin' an' fightin'.' He paused, maybe to give me time to think. 'We're askin' you, Mr Ross, to be that peace-officer,' he said, quietly.

'Well I'll be doggoned,' was all I could find to say and when I'd said it I just stood there not knowing what else to say, and with all of them watching me in a kind of hang-dog way, as if their very lives depended on me. I gave a short laugh.

'Look, gentlemen,' I said. 'I figure you've got me all wrong. The last thing I could be is a peace-officer. I've spent most of my life on the wrong side of the law. I've been mixed up with outlaws. I've killed men. I've been on the run. I don't reckon I'm a fit candidate for your tin star.'

Well, they just stood staring at me with pain and disappointment in their eyes and what I wanted to do was to bawl at them that I wanted none of their law and order. That I just wanted to live my own life. But I couldn't say it. Instead, I said, 'Look, you'll have to give me a lot of time to think about your offer. It's got me kind of off balance. I'll sleep on it and tell you tomorrow.'

'Right,' said David Abraham. 'That's fair

enough, Mr Ross. You go sleep on it and give us your answer tomorrow.'

'That's right' and 'Yessir' chorused the other townsfolk. They made me feel pretty low. You see my plan was to sneak out of that hotel at sun-up and put a couple of hundred miles between myself and Pitchfork before I climbed out of my saddle again.

And that's the idea I went to bed with in The Cattleman's House. It seemed to me a good one and I slept on it well and true. So doggone well that the next thing I knew was sunlight pouring in through my window and a lot of confused noise and hullabaloo drifting up from the street below it. I didn't like the sound of it at all.

Anyway I doused my head in water from a ewer and dug my razor out of my saddle bag. I took my time and a good half-hour later I ambled downstairs and into the dining-room. They served me breakfast the best part of which was the coffee. Then I rolled myself a smoke and prepared for trouble. I could tell it was coming from the noise outside and by the anxious looks of the waitress who looked after me.

I was just enjoying the first pull on my cigarette when the door burst open and Ed Morgan came in. He looked wild and scared. He spotted me at once and came over. He stopped by my chair and stood staring at me.

'The Urquhart crew's come into town,' he said. 'There's Matt Enders, Jess Antrim and about twenty riders. They've got the news about Urquhart. They say we done it. They're talking wild. Anything could happen.'

'Where are they now?' I asked.

'They've gone into The North Platte. Once they've tucked away a few shots of red-eye, there's no knowing what they'll start.'

'It's still none of my affair,' I pointed out.

'They'll tear the town apart,' Ed Morgan pleaded. 'The folks here are helpless without some leader.'

I stood up.

'Look,' I said. 'I'm not buying into this

game. There's too much at stake. But I'll do what I can to stop them making trouble.'

'Mr Ross,' he said. 'If you can do just that this town'll be for ever in your debt.'

'I don't want anyone in my debt,' I said. 'I just want to live a quiet life.'

I led the way out of the dining-room through the foyer where a pale young man stood nervously eating his fingernails and out on to the boardwalk. A small group of townsfolk stood in the centre of the dusty main street. They were arguing loudly, one of them pointing wildly at The North Platte Saloon. I looked down street at the saloon and saw the long line of ponies tied up to the rail. There were a lot of them, flicking their tails in the morning sunshine and an occasional head tossing up. It wouldn't be the horses that'd do the harm. Only the men who rode them.

I went on down into the street and joined the group of townspeople. The men who'd been in The Cattleman's House the night before were all there and a few others.

They stared at me as one.

'I've promised Ed Morgan I'll do what I can,' I said. 'But I'm not wearing any star.' I let that sink well in. 'I ride on once they've gone.'

'All right, Mr Ross,' Abraham said. 'We'll be beholden to you even for that.'

'And now,' I said, 'you'll do what I say and no arguments.'

'Anything you say, Mr Ross,' said Gabbit the liveryman.

'First off I want you all to go and arm yourselves with guns, rifles, anything you've got that'll fire.'

They looked pretty dubious and Abraham said, 'We don't know one end of a gun from the other.'

'There's always time to learn,' I said, cheerfully. 'Meantime I'll ask you, Mr Gabbit, to go over there and collect their ponies. Get some help and run 'em out of town a mile or so.'

Gabbit looked scared to death. 'Go on,' I said. 'They're still busy drinking up courage.'

With a look of desperation he went away and three other men with him.

'The rest of you,' I said, 'once you've got your guns, post yourselves on both sides of the street in windows, on roof-tops, where you like. Wait till I wipe my face with my hand, then let your guns show and make a bit of noise doing it. The rest should be easy.'

They moved away, three of them in the direction of Sloan's gun-shop. I figured maybe they'd dig up enough rifles and six-guns to make some kind of a show but I wasn't too optimistic. They weren't trail-hands or miners or mule-skinners who'd have been tough enough to do what I asked and get a kick out of it. They were just ordinary citizens who'd found their way out West in wagon trains or on the railroad hoping for a quiet life and a chance to do better for themselves than they'd done back East.

Then I was aware that I was alone in the middle of the street. There was a movement among the ponies packed outside The North Platte. I saw them begin to move. There was one rider up on one of them, then another and before you could say 'Jig' the whole bunch of twenty or more were moving quietly down and away from town. Not bad for a beginning, I thought. I watched them and their little sunlit dust-cloud move slowly, very slowly it seemed, out of sight. This was going to cause a lot of bother when the Urquhart hands came out of the saloon.

I looked around and saw a window go up in the barber-shop next to the small saloon called The Trail. Something that looked like the barrel of a gun glinted briefly in the opening. Then I saw another movement up on the flat roof of Ed Morgan's feed and grain store. It was even more heartening. It was an arm waving a rifle.

The sun was climbing well up now and I was beginning to feel its effect. Sweat drops formed on my forehead and before moving my hand to wipe them off, I remembered the signal we'd arranged. I'd have to leave wiping my face for a while till the Urquhart crew showed up. Excitement began to build up in me. I could feel it in the pit of my stomach, in my leg-muscles. If they didn't come out soon I was going to be in a bad way.

And then they showed. Just the first of them, a tall, gangling hombre who slouched out of The North Platte and stood there in the sunlight staring at the empty tie-rails in front of the saloon. Then it seemed to dawn upon him and he turned back, moving quickly into the saloon. I heard his yell and tensed myself for the result. It came fast. The Urquhart crew came out through the batwing doors with a rush. They paused on the boardwalk, taking in what had happened and then someone must have seen me standing alone in the middle of the street. They stopped talking and all stared at me. It was a mighty queer feeling, standing there, with twenty pairs of wild, hostile eyes glaring at me. I could see Jess Antrim, Urquhart's foreman, in the front. He said something to them then and they came trooping out in my direction.

I stood my ground, waiting till they weren't more than twenty feet away from me. Then I made a nice smooth draw.

I said, 'That's far enough, gents. Let's have a little pow-wow with a bit of space to move in. I hate being crowded.'

I don't think they'd expected me to draw because they stopped dead in their tracks, spreading out a bit and looking more than a mite surprised.

Jess Antrim, with a mean look in his eye took a step forward.

'What's happened to our hosses?' His tone was flat, heavy, threatening.

'Someone took 'em away,' I said.

His face reddened and I knew he was pretty near boiling over.

'Why?' The one word seemed to come out with difficulty.

'I kind of figured things might be easier for all if you were without 'em for a while.'

I had him buffaloed and the small army of Urquhart's hands behind him, including Matt Enders, his beard a little longer than when I'd seen him the night before. Strange little things a man will notice at times like that. I noticed just then not only that his beard was longer but that his right hand was sliding gently down towards the gun hanging low against his leg.

'Keep your hands away from that hogleg, Mr Enders,' I said. 'I'd hate to see you with only two fingers 'stead of the usual five.'

His hand started moving upwards again. And Jess Antrim looking colder and angrier every second, said, 'Let's cut the cackle, friend. I reckon it's time to see your cards.'

'They're all around you,' I said and wiped my face with what's left of my right hand. There were faint sounds from my hidden supporters, clear and unmistakable in the quiet morning air – the click of a hammer being pulled back, a rattle, a squeaking window going up. The Urquhart crew stared around and saw the gun-barrels poking out of windows, the signs of ambush, and some of them looked kind of sick.

'Looks like you've caught us on the hop,' said Antrim, after one bleak survey of the fortified landscape.

'That was the idea,' I said modestly. 'All we want is for you and your crew to ride on out of Pitchfork peaceable-like.'

'There's a thing we'd know before we ride out,' said Antrim. 'And that's who killed Ed Urquhart?'

'I can't answer that,' I said. 'But I can tell you one thing. It wasn't any of the towns-people. I was with most of 'em in The Cattleman's House. Riders came into town. There were a few shots and they rode off after dumping the body on our doorstep. We went out and brought him in but he was dead when we got to him. That's all there is to it.'

He stared at me for what seemed a long time, his pale blue eyes penetrating into me for the possible lie. I looked back at him and at last he threw up his hands in a gesture of failure. There was something likeable about Jess Antrim at that moment. Maybe it was his loyalty to the dead rancher. Maybe there was something in him that answered to something in me.

Then Matt Enders shoved his big bearded face forward.

'How're we to know you ain't tellin' a pack of lies, mister?'

'You'll just have to take my word for it,' I said.

'Your word,' he said and spat onto the rutted dusty street.

There was a faint stir and a muttering noise in the group behind him. I braced myself for trouble but Antrim stopped it.

'We'll take Ed back to the ranch,' he said. 'Maybe you can get someone to lend us a wagon and maybe collect our hosses too.'

I turned away, holstering my gun, not without a kind of prickling feeling between my shoulder-blades, and made a signal towards where I figured some of the townsfolk would be. I also shouted to them to come on out.

This they did, slow, reluctant and awkward-looking at first, then gradually easing up as they realised they weren't going to be gunned down. Ed Morgan was among the first.

I said, 'They're taking Urquhart's body back to the ranch. They'll need a flat-bed wagon and their mounts. You get 'em here.'

'Right,' said Morgan and went off.

Jess Antrim sent some of his crew to fetch the body of Urquhart and the rest of us stood around in the morning sunlight with mighty little to say to each other. Fortunately the wagon appeared in a couple of minutes and then they were all busy putting the dead rancher in it and sorting out their ponies.

When they were at last ready and mounted Jess Antrim wheeled his horse round to where I was standing.

He looked down at me.

'Don't think this is all over an' done with,' he said, bitterly. 'I've got a pretty good notion who did it an' when we know for certain God help him or them. I'll wipe 'em out like I would a rattler.'

'You'd better be sure,' I said. 'And remember that when you start this business of wiping out other folks, you may all get wiped out together. Maybe thataway this Basin'll get a little peace.'

He looked like he might say more but instead he pulled his mouth into a thin hard line and after one more cold stare at me he said simply, 'Let's go.' They got into motion all at once and for a moment I thought it was going to be a nice peaceful orderly exodus from town. It just wasn't in the nature of that bunch of cowhands to go out quietly even when they were escort to a corpse. Someone in the close-packed group let out a yell, the wild yell of the confederate cavalry, the driver of the wagon whipped up his horses and they were all off at a dead run.

It was then that it happened. Even as the Urquhart band reached the end of the street a homesteader's wagon came out of a turning into their path. Whatever hit it maybe we'll never know but only seconds later it had keeled over in the dust of their passing and lay there with its off wheels spinning and someone inside screaming.

I raced down the street towards it. The Urquhart crew were no more than a cloud of dust in the distance. I got to the wagon and peered inside. There was a woman inside and what looked like a child. Townsfolk came up and we got them out. The woman was nothing more than frightened but the boy was badly hurt. His right leg had been crushed in the fall and looked broken. He was not more than six or seven years old.

Well, we got him into Abraham's house and Mrs Abraham got to work on the broken leg. We all trooped out then into the street and something that had been building up in me came out.

'I'll be your peace-officer,' I said. 'I reckon this place needs someone if it's only to protect the women and children.'

'That's mighty good of you, Mr Ross,' said

Abraham and others shook my hand and patted me on the back.

They found me a one-room shack at the end of town and promised to run up a solid building with a cell for malefactors and such and Gabbit the liveryman said he'd make me a star in his forge.

Next day I swore on a Bible to enforce the laws of the United States and keep the peace in the town of Pitchfork.

'But remember this,' I said. 'To keep the peace here I'll have to keep an eye on the Urquhart crew and on the Cartledges and their friends up in the hills. It's them who'll bust up your peace and it's them who've got to learn not to take the law into their own hands. As I see it my first job is to ride over to the Urquhart place and see that they don't go gunning for the homesteaders.'

And that was how it began with me on Bessie riding out of town to the Urquhart spread.

CHAPTER FOUR

It was near noon when I rode out of town. I was soon out on rolling grassland and heading east to where I'd been told the Urquhart ranch lay. It was fine and warm and I sang a song or two to keep myself company. I tried a few verses of 'The Dying Cowboy' but after a time it petered out and I found myself singing 'Beautiful Dreamer' – a mighty nice song that had worked its way all over the West in the years after the war. It seemed to please Bessie, my mare, too, and she ambled on her way contentedly – a bit of a dreamer herself, come to think of it.

The trail east of Pitchfork was pretty clearly marked. It wound over a small rise and along the flank of a ridge. There was a good view of the Basin from there and I pulled up under a clump of cottonwoods to have a look at it. The only thing that troubled me was a small ball of dust rolling swiftly westwards and about a couple of miles from where I stood. A rider or maybe two in a hurry. Cutting across the wide flat acres of the Basin towards the hills where the homesteaders and their dubious pals were probably hatching up more trouble. It was them who'd put paid to Ed Urquhart's account I figured, and started something that would take much longer a-dying than Urquhart did.

I watched the dust-ball roll away until it was lost in the folds of the foothills. Then I gave old Bessie the word and we trundled on. We'd gone about a mile and ahead of us lay a wide patch of cottonwoods. I could see some rocky outcrops just south of them and the trail lay straight towards them. I don't know what sixth sense warned me that I wasn't alone in that neck of the woods but no sooner did the warning come than I circled off the trail and up into the shelter of the rocks. It wasn't any too soon. I'd just got Bessie tucked away behind a shoulder of rock when I heard the 'clop-clop' of hoofs. I got well into the corner and stared down at the trail about thirty feet away from me. They came into sight. A bunch of five, well mounted and armed to the eyebrows, let alone the teeth. I stared and then almost shouted in amazement. Three rode by and I didn't know 'em from Adam. Number four was Al Rachell. I wasn't mistaken. The fifth horseman was an old acquaintance and I'd last seen him through a veil of gunsmoke back in Newtown. His name was Lew Owens and that wasn't long after I'd killed his brother, Brad.

Well it wasn't a moment for a friendly get-together so I kept well back with Bessie in the shelter of the rock and watched the five men ride on. They seemed to be heading towards Pitchfork but they would almost certainly be making for the hill ranches of the Cartledges and their friends.

When the dust of their passing had begun

to settle I led Bessie out of our hidey-hole, climbed on board and rode on towards the Urquhart spread.

Lew Owens. We'd met up in a saloon in Newtown over a year ago, the three Owens brothers, Brad, Lew and Will, and a fourth man whose name was Jed Benson. We'd liquored up a spell and fell to playing poker. The game went easy for a while and then suddenly it hotted up with the best cards coming my way. All this seemed fine to me but it didn't go down well with Brad Owens. He just got madder and madder as the dollars came my way. I could smell trouble coming and decided to quit the game. I said I'd had enough and I leant forward and collected my winnings. It was then that Brad Owens's temper boiled over. He yelled something about a tinhorn gambler and went for his gun. Someone shouted 'No' and I kicked the table we'd been playing on right into the laps of the other three. Brad Owens's gun exploded and I drew. He fired again, wild, and I shot him. He spun round once and then fell flat on his face. I backed away towards the exit and a solitary gun went into action. I fired back and again the gun roared. This time I could see who was firing. It was the one they called Jed Benson. His third shot hit me as I reached the bat-wing doors of the saloon. It struck my gun hand knocking the Colt away and sending a scream of pain along my nerves. I did the only thing left for me to do. I shot out through the doors, vaulted into the saddle of Bessie and went out of town on a dead run. That was the last I'd seen of the Owens boys until now. Riding slowly along in the warm sunshine I looked down at what was left of my right hand. It had healed up all right and I'd learned to use my left instead but things had never been quite the same since without it.

I'd never had any illusions about the Owens brothers or Jed Benson. They were well known in parts of Arizona for their skill with rope and branding-iron on other men's cows and I wondered now why one of them was visiting Wyoming. I figured it wasn't for any sociable reason. Lew Owens would be here for one thing only – cash. How'd he get it? Not by digging. Maybe from the Cartledges, maybe from the Urquharts. I reckoned if I rode on and was patient I'd soon find out.

Ride on I did and at the end of another thirty minutes I came to a trail that led downgrade towards a large-scale ranch about a mile away. This was the Urquhart spread. It couldn't be anything else. It was just about big enough for a man like Urquhart or Miss Urquhart. Coming closer I could see the lay-out and mighty impressive it was. There was a good-sized house with a veranda around two sides of it nicely placed in front of a stand of cottonwoods. Angling off from it were farm-buildings, bunkhouses, a forge and cattle pens. I was about half a mile away and there didn't seem to be a soul about.

I went on in, right into the yard and called out 'Hallo, the house,' and no one answered. Over to the right a track led off over a rise and something made me ride Bessie over thataway. I got to the top of the rise and then I knew why the ranch had been empty. I could see the whole thing from where I was. The ring of men standing bareheaded in the morning sun, the faint murmur of a voice, the hole in the ground. They were only two hundred yards away and they were burying Ed Urquhart.

It wasn't the moment for me to horn in but I've never been able to pick the right moment for anything, not even the moment of being born. I moseyed down to where the burial was going on. I slung Bessie's reins round a branch close to where the Urquhart hands had left their mounts. Then I took off my hat and waited respectful-like until the ceremony was over.

It didn't take long. There was a movement in the crowd of thirty or so around the grave. The crowd opened up and the figure of Miss Urquhart stood facing me. She wasn't dressed as a boy any longer and was wearing some kind of dark dress and over her head she wore a little black mantilla.

She was a beautiful sight on that fine sunny morning but a mighty sad one. Slowly she began to walk towards me as if coming to me was the natural thing to do. The rest of them followed close behind her. About four paces away from me she stopped. I was shocked by what I saw in her face. She was white with grief and maybe something else. She looked ten years older and a hundred times angrier than when I'd faced her up on the hills.

'What are you doing here and what's that thing you've got pinned on to your vest?' The voice that asked the questions was dulled with pain but she wanted an answer.

'I've come about the killing of your Pa,' I said. 'This thing on my vest is a badge of office. The folks down in Pitchfork seemed to think they wanted a feller to look after their interests an' they chose me.'

'You!' she said and gave a short dry laugh with a big edge of scorn to it. 'Why you?'

'Ma'am,' I said, 'I don't rightly know. But when your riders hightailed it out of town yesterday they knocked over a homesteader's wagon and broke a small boy's leg. Maybe the citizens of Pitchfork need a little protection.'

For a moment something – a thought, an impulse, a woman's true nature clouded her eyes and my spirits rose. Then almost as quickly they sank way down into my boots. She pulled her mouth into a thin, hard line and said, 'You dare to talk about protection for those fat storekeepers when my father lies there, dead and buried. Get off my ranch before I kill you – you and your tin star.'

I looked straight into her blazing eyes.

'There's been enough killing,' I said.

'There'll be more to come.'

'Not if I can stop it,' I countered. 'I came across to ask you and your men to let things ride for the time. I'll find your Pa's murderer and the law'll see he hangs for it. More than that a man can't say.'

'You've come too late,' she said, bitterly. 'We'll find who killed my father and when we do we'll punish him as he deserves.'

'Let me throw him out,' said someone behind her and looking up I recognised the big brutal figure of Matt Enders.

'No,' she said sharply. 'We'll do this properly.' She looked at me again. 'You can get off my land, Mr Ross, and go back where you belong. Don't ever come here again. If you do you will be shot down.' They were terrible words to hear coming from a young girl. I said one last word.

'If you take the law into your own hands, ma'am, there's no knowing where the trouble will end and how many innocent folks will suffer. I ask you for the last time to let me handle this the proper way.'

She just stared at me and then said slowly, 'Get out.'

There didn't seem very much else I could do right then. My Pa used to say, 'You can argify with another man, a hoss or a cow but you only come to grief if you argify with a woman.'

With my Pa's words in my ears I turned

away to Bessie and very slowly I climbed into the leather.

I stood there a moment looking at all of them standing grim and silent in the morning sunshine. Then I gave Bessie the word and we rode away over the rise, past the big ranch-house and out into the valley.

I wasn't quite certain what my next move was to be. It ought to be over in the direction of the Cartledge layout where maybe I could pick up some kind of indication as to who had gunned down Ed Urquhart. But that could wait a bit, I argued. I'd ride back to town and do a bit of thinking before I got any deeper in. The whole thing was building up into an all too familiar pattern. Big ranch folk start treading on the small hill people. Small hill people start recruiting – not just friends or neighbours, anyone, gunslingers, outlaws, the riff-raff who had spread all over the West since the war ended, living off other folks, like the boll-weevil lives off the cotton plant. The feud spreads. Folks are dry-gulched. It was a well-known story. And it was an ugly one.

Bessie jogged on quietly in the general direction of the town of which I was now the properly elected peace-officer. It was a mighty peculiar thought. Johnny Ross – ex-cowhand, ex-gambler, ex-outlaw, and now marshal of a cow-town in the Wyoming hills. It took some believing. Maybe, kind of sooner than later, he'd be an ex-peace-officer too.

The outskirts of Pitchfork were a few tar and paper shacks edging the broad trail into town. It was a trail well worn by the hoofs of cattle, and horses, by wagon-wheels – an old town by Western standards. Someone had told me the day before that it was close on three years old. I looked along the trail and it was as empty as a trail through the desert. There wasn't a soul in sight, just as if they'd all fled. I rode on pondering some and as I got closer in I saw just one sign of life – five horses standing hipshot outside the saloon called The Cattleman's House. That would be Lew Owens, Al Rachell and the other three riders I'd seen on my way out to the Urquhart spread.

It was a pretty grim prospect but you can't live by avoiding showdowns. If a showdown was to come now I figured I'd better face it. I brought Bessie to a stop outside the saloon and flung her reins round the tie-rail which the other cayuses weren't using. No sense in getting your hoss all mixed up with others.

I hitched my gunbelt into its proper position. Then I took a gander around me. The street looked even emptier than before, but over the way in the window of Morgan's feed and grain store a curtain moved. That was all. I figured that there were lots more folk standing quietly behind curtains at that moment, their eyes fixed on me and the way into the saloon. I could almost feel their stare on my back as I ambled up the steps on to the boardwalk and in through the bat-wing doors of the saloon.

The big room with its long bar contained eight men. Behind the bar the bar-keep stood, his hands flat down on the polished mahogany top. He looked up in my direction as I came in. Not quite facing him and strung out along the bar stood five men. Their heads swivelled round slowly a little after the barman. Lew Owens was nearest the door. Rachell somewhere about the middle. Out in the centre of the room two of the men who'd helped make me peace-officer sat at a table. They were Joe Humphress and Mike Channing.

I walked over to the bar. The bartender sidled in my direction.

'Evenin', Mr Ross.'

'Evenin',' I said. 'They say whisky's good for a ridin' man's throat. I'll have one.'

He produced a bottle and a shot-glass and pushed them towards me. I turned round towards where Humphress and Channing were sitting.

'Maybe you gents would care to join me in a snort?' I said. Was I being just sociable or looking for help in a time of trouble? They exchanged looks and then Channing mumbled:

'Reckon it's kinda late, Mr Ross. Some other time, if you don't mind.'

'Sure,' I said.

They stood up and moseyed off towards the door, slowly, but not too slowly. The bat-wings swung to and fro behind them. I picked up the bottle and filled the shot-glass. No sound, no movement from the five jaspers on my right. I raised the glass and drank and a voice came whispering dry and deadly along the bar-top.

'Mister Ross. Now ain't that mighty peculiar. No one down in the Arizona territory knew him as anything other than Johnny.' It was Lew Owens, of course. He'd figured I hadn't seen him and probably thought he'd really got me below the water-line. I didn't look at them. I gave myself another snort of whisky instead.

'Every man's entitled to settle down and be known as Mister, Lew Owens,' I said, and went on. 'But that ain't neither here nor there. What's more to the point is why you're a-struttin' round up here in Wyoming so far away from your usual dunghill.'

I turned a little towards them as I spoke. You can't be very much in command of a situation when you sit sideways to it. I could see them all now and had the advantage of them. Only the nearest of the bunch, Lew Owens, was favourably placed.

He said in that dry whispering voice of his, 'Still the same cocky little rooster, ain't you, Johnny? Still ready to gun yore way outa trouble. Only this time you've got a tin star to hide behind.'

'Any time you want to come a-smokin',' I said, 'I'll take my badge off first and still have time to outshoot you, Lew Owens.'

'Gents,' said the barman and then stopped short as if he couldn't quite think of what to say. The situation was warming up and a small cold premonitory shiver ran down my spine.

'Talk!' said a voice from beyond Owens and a figure tall and gangling and unknown to me slid out of the group and stood crouching slightly, right hand like a claw hovering over the gunbutt low down on his right leg. 'Fill your hand, Mr Ross.'

I did as I was bid but the stranger's gun had cleared leather seconds before mine. His gun roared and the shot went whistling somewhere just above my head. I took a little more time, fired and hit him in the right arm. The distance was no more than twenty feet and my shot spun him round like a top. He fell heavily. I waited. The rest of the bunch made nary a movement.

'Better have a look at your pal, gents,' I said. 'Maybe he needs a little attention.'

They went to him then, picked him up and found the damage I'd inflicted.

'You've ventilated his right arm,' said Al Rachell, accusingly.

'Well,' I said, 'what did you expect me to do? Comb his hair?'

They stood there uncertain, caught off balance as it were and I pressed my advantage, with a boldness I didn't really feel.

'Go on. Go on,' I said. 'Git out of here or I'll lock the lot of you up in the hoosegow for breakin' the peace.'

'This ain't the time now,' said Lew Owens. 'We'll settle with you later, Johnny.'

'Any time at all,' I said airily.

'Git him outa here,' said Owens and between them they assisted the wounded man out of the saloon.

I waited, a mite anxiously. There was nothing to stop any of them dry-gulching me from a window but I figured they'd be too busy and might even have some other plan in mind. There was a vague murmur of voices from outside and then silence for several minutes. They were still there but I reckoned they must be tying up their wounded pal's arm. Then suddenly there was the sound of horses in movement. A gun roared and a window fell in with a crash. In the silence that followed I could hear the drum of hoofs fading into the distance. Then more silence. Faintly embarrassed I stood up behind the bar. I couldn't quite remember how I'd got there. The barman also climbed into view. I went round to my proper side.

'Reckon I could do with another snort,' I said.

'Yeah,' observed the barman. 'Gunsmoke kinda makes a man thirsty.' I poured myself a drink and was pushing the bottle towards the barman when the bat-wing doors behind me were pushed open. I leaped round like a frightened deer and found myself with my gun in my hand pointing straight at Mike Channing's fat stomach.

He made a gesture of denial and seemed to be trying to say something but the words didn't come.

Slowly I let the tension ease out of me.

'Don't ever do that again,' I croaked.

'We heard gunfire,' said Humphress. 'We thought we'd better find out what's going on.'

'That was some time ago,' I said. 'There's no call for you to be scairt now. They've gone.'

'We're not scared,' Humphress said lamely. 'We … we…'

'You just stayed outa range.' I finished the

words for him. 'You elected me as your marshal. All right. I've been carrying out my duties. Now you can go off to bed and sleep the sleep of the just.'

CHAPTER FIVE

For two days after the meeting with Lew
Owens and the others in The Cattleman's
House I did nothing much, a form of activity
I've always been pretty keen on and pretty
good at. After all, the citizens of Pitchfork
were paying me to be their peace-officer, and
not to go wandering off into the Wyoming
rangelands looking for trouble. If trouble
came to town then I was paid sixty dollars a
month to deal with it. So I just sat on a
rocker outside the saloon in the late autumn
sunshine and chewed the fat with one or two
gents who seemed to be in like case to
myself. One of them was Tom Roselaw, pro-
prietor of The Cattleman's House. He was a
lean coyote-faced hombre with long drooping moustaches and a restless manner. He'd
wander out on to the boardwalk and stand

around talking for a ten-minute stretch. Then he'd suddenly look worried and mosey off back to the saloon. He let on that he too had come up the trail but when I asked where from he shut up like a clam, put on his worried-man look and sloped off inside.

Howsomever, in one way or another, and coming out in neat little ten-minute parcels, he managed to provide a whole lot of information about the general set-up in and around Pitchfork, including his fellow citizens and their families, the Urquharts and the Cartledges and the nameless ones who'd been drifting around since high summer.

'Could be they're just cowhands lookin' for work. Could be.' He looked down at me. 'I figure they're after something bigger than rustlin' cows out on the Red Butte plateau. When I first saw you, Mr Ross, I figured you was after something bigger than punchin' cows.' His eyes staring down at me were full of dark and furtive speculation.

'I've done my share of cow-punchin',' I said dryly.

'Yes,' he said softly. 'I know.'

I stood up.

'How do you know what I've done?' I said.

His eyes shifted away.

'It was just a manner of speaking, Mr Ross. I reckon I meant to say "I guess so", not "I know".'

'You'd better watch what you say. One of these days you'll say "I know" to the wrong hombre and then you might be sorry.'

'Yes,' he said, looking very anxious and worried indeed and was off into his saloon like a gopher down its hole.

This little chat took place around three o'clock on the second day of my inactivity. I decided then that I'd had enough of rocker-sitting and waiting for something to happen. I was making ready for an afternoon's pasear around the countryside by working my way through a hunk of steak and a heap of fried potatoes when who should sidle up to me again but Tom Roselaw.

Bending low over my table, he said, in a hoarse whisper:

101

'Thought you might like to know that somethin's cookin' on the Urquhart ranch, Mr Ross.'

'Somethin's been cookin' in here,' I said through a mouthful of potato, 'an I'm sure tryin' to appreciate it.' I finished the potato. 'What are you tryin' to tell me, Mr Roselaw?'

'I don't know for sure, Mr Ross,' he said, limply. 'But if pressed, I'd say the Urquharts are going to make the Cartledges pay for killing Ed Urquhart.'

'Who says the Cartledges killed Ed Urquhart?' My voice was pretty stern.

'Rumour hath it,' he said, avoiding my eyes.

'Rumour's been called a lying horse,' I said and stood up. 'Reckon it's time I put an end to some of these rumours. Time to ride.'

'Where?' The question was as soft and innocent as an angel's breath.

'Here an' there,' I replied. 'Just here an' there.' Somehow or other I felt about as much trust for Mr T Roselaw as I would for a Gila monster.

I left the saloon and walked back to my little shack or Marshal's Office, as the notice said over the door. I picked up my gunbelt and my Winchester, and walked the hop, skip and a jump to the livery stable where Bessie had been spending a few quiet dignified hours ministered to by Tad Gabbit.

After a few words I managed to get Bessie saddled and out of the stable. Then I climbed aboard and we moseyed slowly out of town. No one seemed to be much concerned about my movements but they were, I figured, remembering Tom Roselaw.

We didn't hurry along the trail to the north rim of the Basin. We rode leisurely, keeping a careful eye on signs of distant movement in the valley. It was the way I'd taken a few days before with young Dan Cartledge and I followed it over to their layout without difficulty. This time however my welcome was different.

The Cartledge house lay in a hollow

103

depression about five miles across the big benchland forming the western edge of the Basin. I could see it about a mile ahead of me. A few hundred yards ahead of me the ground rose sharply on my left in a rock-studded knob. As I was a passing it a voice called out:

'Hold it, mister, or I'll let daylight through you.'

It was a young voice, kind of high and excited and I figured I knew whose voice it was.

'Now why would you be wantin' to let daylight through me, Dan Cartledge?' I yelled back.

It was enough. He came out from behind a large rock about thirty feet up the hillside, looking sheepish and carrying a big old Sharps buffalo gun. Old maybe but good enough to put a hole through me like a railway tunnel.

'Kinda failed to recognise you, Mr Ross,' he said.

'Good thing I introduced myself,' I said.

'That's a mighty dangerous weapon you're a-carrying, son.'

'What you doin' up here on the Bench, Mr Ross?' His voice had suddenly gone cold. 'Thought you'd gone over to the Urquharts.'

'I don't go over to anyone,' I said with equal coldness. 'I figure I'm better off if I ride alone.'

'Yeah,' he said with a kind of sigh in his voice. 'Not much good comes of bein' on one side or t'other.' He looked up at me. 'You comin' into the house, Mr Ross?'

'Yep,' I said. 'I'd like a word with your Pa, if he's home. Any of his friends around?'

'Which friends?' His voice went suddenly shrill.

'I had in mind Rachell, Point and Gillams,' I said. 'You may remember I met 'em when I visited with you a day or two ago.'

'No, they ain't there,' said Dan. 'They got a place over to Bear Crick.' His voice was harsh with dislike or something stronger.

'Let's go then,' I said and gave Bessie the word.

'My pony's on the other side of the butte,' said Dan and walked off. I followed slowly and caught up with him a few minutes later. Together we rode down the slight slope to the house.

Ep Cartledge was swinging a big axe into a tree branch just left of the house. He stopped as we rode in and stood there, a tall commanding figure, his big beard jutting out truculently.

We climbed down and hitched the horses to a fence.

'Well?' His voice matched his bulk.

'I've come over to ask you to use some savvy an' stop this feud with the Urquharts,' I said without hanky-pankying around the point.

I could see him eyeing my marshal's star and he went on doing so for a long moment before he answered.

'I'm a man of peace,' he said at last. 'I also have a respect for the law.'

'Did you have a hand in the killing of Ed Urquhart, Mr Cartledge?' I said.

He stared at me wide-eyed. His mouth opened and shut and no word came. He dropped the axe and came towards me.

'I knew not that he had been killed,' he said.

'So be it,' I said. 'But I figure some of your friends certainly know about it. I mean Rachell, Point and Gillams,' I said. 'And a jigger called Owens.'

He stared at me without speaking and his eyes were empty of all guile.

'They should not have done it,' he said and his voice had dropped to a whisper. 'It was not for them to take the law into their own hands.'

'I reckon law doesn't mean much to any of 'em,' I said. 'You'd do well to have no more truck with any of them. They'll only bring grief to you and yours.'

'Yes,' said Ephraim Cartledge. He shook himself as if getting rid of some unpleasant or unwelcome thought.

'Come into my house and my woman will give you refreshment,' he said. We went into the house and Mrs Cartledge greeted us.

There was a rocker near the fireplace which I hadn't seen on my previous visit.

'Sit you there,' said Mrs Cartledge, indicating the rocker.

I did as I was bid. The Cartledge folk weren't the kind you argued with or even made social small talk with. She was pouring black coffee out of a big black pot into three tin mugs. She handed me one and indicated a tin of molasses.

'Help yourself, Mr Ross,' she said.

The mug was half-way to my mouth when the first shot cut loose and a window left of the door shattered into fragments. There was a half-stifled cry from Mrs Cartledge but for a few seconds we just sat or stood frozen into immobility. Then I seemed to wake up.

'Get down,' I yelled.

It was lucky we did. The solitary shot was followed by a barrage of shooting. Windows came in. Slugs thudded into the walls, the door and through the window into the wall behind us.

I was lying close in under the window, my Colt in my left hand and cursing my stupidity in leaving my Winchester in its sheath still on Bessie. Dan had taken the horses into a barn before following me into the house.

I edged my way up the log wall until I could get a view of the ranch yard. It was as dark as your hat now with an occasional flash of muzzle light as one or other of the besiegers popped off in the general direction of the house. None of it was very accurate but then ranchhands are often no great shakes at shooting. The word 'ranchhands' had come quite naturally into my mind, because I'd assumed from the first shot that it was the Urquhart outfit that was gunning around out there in the darkness. I hadn't been wide of the mark in this because a moment later I heard a voice yell out something and I'd have bet seven hundred dollars it was the voice of Jess Antrim.

I heard a noise then over to my right and

looking up saw old man Cartledge lumbering to his feet like an angry bear.

'What in hell d'you think you're a-doin'?' I asked coldly.

'I'm going out there to smite the Philistine hip and thigh,' he roared at me.

'Why, you stupid old jackass,' I said, now feeling more than a mite riled, 'they'd shoot you down before you'd got six feet from your own front door. Get down an' ride this out.'

I don't know what he did then because there was a lot more shooting and yelling from outside and suddenly I was aware of the acrid stink of burning over to my left. I couldn't be sure at first and then after one quick look I knew. They'd fired the barn. This made me good and mad because Bessie was in there and I wasn't having my mare burned to a crisp by a lot of good-for-nothing sons.

I looked round for Dan.

'Is there a way out back?' I shouted.

'Through the door,' he yelled.

'Keep 'em busy,' I said, and went on out the way he'd indicated. There was a small kitchen and wash-up and a door. I opened it slowly and came face to face with a man of about my own size. I was quicker. I pistol-whipped him with the barrel of my Colt and he sank down quietly at my feet. I stepped over him and went along the back of the house in a crouch. When I reached the angle I could see the barn, with its roof on fire. Someone must have tossed a light on to it and it was now blazing brightly. There might well be a back way in, I figured, and I ran towards the rear end. There was a small entrance and no door. I went in. I could hear the horses stamping around and whinnying with fright as smoke and sparks came down into the barn. Already a big bale of hay was smouldering just to my left.

There was only one way out of there for the horses and that was the way they'd come in. I crawled forward through the thickening smoke and found Dan's pony, Bessie my mare and three other broncs all circling, pawing the ground and generally showing signs of anxiety.

'O.K, my beauties,' I said and moving forward I slipped their tie-ropes one by one. 'Out,' I yelled and fired a shot just over their ears. They bunched, whirled and stampeded for the entrance. Bessie, I noted with brief pride, was a neck ahead of the others. I hoped I'd see her again. She meant a whole lot to me.

My next move was to get back to the house so I returned through the smoke to the hole I'd come in by. I crawled out keeping my eyes at work but the Urquhart crew still hadn't tried to take the house. I saw a couple of shots coming from one of the windows. The firing from the besiegers seemed to have died away. I wondered why. The answer came quick. A whole new burst of firing suddenly came from deeper into the darkness. There was some broken shooting from nearer in to me and then a voice yelled, high and excited:

'All right. All right. Git out of hyar, Circle U.'

There was some more shooting. Someone let out a high-pitched cry and this was followed by some confused shouting. It sure looked as if Circle U had got themselves nicely boxed-in. Not for long. A moment's silence was broken by the unmistakable drumming of hooves. They came out of the trees in the vague light cast by the burning barn. And they rode straight towards me, firing kind of wild. I slipped back into the barn and the whole bunch whirled past and away into the night.

I came out and ran fast to the house. The door in back was still open and I ran in and then as I reached the room in which I had left the Cartledges I stopped short. There was a body lying in the middle of the room. Crouched over it was the figure of Mrs Cartledge and kneeling at its head was Ep Cartledge, his hands clasped as if in prayer but no word came from him. His eyes were fixed and staring up at the roof. Neither of them took any note of me and the boy lying on the floor looked as if he'd never note anything ever again. I went over to them.

'Mrs Cartledge,' I said.

She looked at me slow-like, and her eyes were dry and empty of everything.

'He's dead,' she said. 'Dead.'

I turned to the father and his eyes moved away from the ceiling and stared at me. It was as if he'd never seen me before. There was something else too in his look. I'd seen it before. I'd seen it years ago. It was after the battle of Shiloh. I'd been out with a picket and we'd picked up a big bearded Yankee captain. He'd gone mad and he looked at us with exactly the same look as I now saw in the eye of Ep Cartledge.

The door came open with a crash and men pushed into the room. The first was Joshua Brill and close at his heels came Lew Owens, Rachell, Point, Gillams and a couple more gents I didn't know. They too stopped short as they took in what had happened.

As if aware of them at last Ep Cartledge lumbered to his feet. He stood there swaying on his feet staring at them as if he wasn't too sure about them either.

He said, 'They that take the sword shall perish by the sword.'

'Yes, sir, Mr Cartledge,' said Jake Gillams. 'Only it won't be the sword, it'll be a gun.'

'Vengeance is mine,' continued Cartledge.

'You've forgotten three other words that ought to come in,' I said. He turned and glared at me.

'Saith the Lord,' I went on. 'He meant, I figure, that if anyone was to go gunning for vengeance, then it was His business and no one else's.'

In the silence that followed I heard the click of the hammer of a gun and then Lew Owens whispered:

'One thing's certain, Johnny Ross. Whoever avenges Dan Cartledge, it sure won't be you.'

'Maybe. Maybe not,' I said, wishing that I hadn't let him get the drop on me.

'Go and get his gun, Al,' said Lew Owens. 'Don't move, Johnny.'

Rachell came over behind me. I didn't

115

move. There was nothing to be gained by doing so, other than a narrow grave just six by three. I felt him lift the gun out of its holster.

'What do we do with him, Lew?' Al Rachell sounded more than a little unsure of himself.

'Let him be.' It was Ep Cartledge speaking. 'He came to us and gave us help in our distress.'

He was still holding his rifle. Lew Owens stared at him, his eyes narrowing.

'Keep outa this, old man,' he said.

Cartledge brought his gun up. 'You shall not harm him under my roof.'

A gun roared suddenly from my left and Cartledge shuddered as the bullet tore into him. He stood swaying for a moment, his eyes staring madly. Then his gun exploded. There was a second shot, this time from Lew Owens. The first had come from Jake Gillams. Then there was a moment's silence; gunsmoke swirled in the low-ceilinged room. Slowly Ep Cartledge crumpled to the ground and we all stood there while scream after scream came from Mrs Cartledge.

Joshua Brill went down on his knees and prayed.

I looked at Lew Owens and then at the rest of his gang.

I said slowly, 'You'll pay for this, all of you, if it takes me to my dying day.'

'That may not be long a-comin',' said Lew Owens and then something crashed into the back of my head and I seemed to fall over and over into a great crying pit of darkness.

CHAPTER SIX

I woke up but it was like I was still asleep and in a nightmare. All I could see was a kind of mist, red mist and all I could do was stare into it, unable to move. I shut my eyes and my memory got to work. The Cartledge house, the raiders, the fire. Maybe it was fire I could see. Then the other happenings came tumbling back; the arrival of Lew Owens and the rest, the death of young Dan and the killing of Ep Cartledge. It was all back now, even the last thing I could remember, the blow on the back of my head.

And now I was awake again. I opened my eyes once more, slow and careful like. They didn't open easily. Like as if there was something sticking to them. Molasses, maybe. Someone must have hit me with a jar of molasses. This struck me as really funny and I made a strange croaking noise.

'Ain't nothin' to laugh at,' said a voice from somewhere roundabout. 'You're in a bad spot, mister, and that's for sure.'

My eyes opened a bit more easily and I could see things at last. A bit vague and wobbly but still things. A pair of boots and some legs. A chair, and still hazy, a large shape sitting in the chair. I figured from the way I was looking at him that I was lying on the floor.

I lay back and rested a while. It didn't seem to matter how long I rested. The only thing that would have improved matters would have been a nice fat goose-feather bed. I tried opening my eyes again and this time it was easier. I could see now. I focused on the hombre in the chair and recognised him. It didn't make things seem any better. It was Al Rachell. He got up as I looked at him and stood towering over me. Like a grizzly bear, I thought but twice as ugly and maybe three times as brutal. To prove my point he kicked me not too gently in the ribs. I reckoned my best play would be to get him off guard so I let out a few groans and shut my eyes. This seemed to satisfy him for the moment and he moved off. I could hear him ambling about the room and from the various little noises he made it looked as if he was doing some cooking. The thought of food put me into no end of a state. I took a quick peep towards the light, saw a window and knew it was daylight. Close on twenty-four hours since I'd eaten. Nothing makes me madder than being kept without food and this soon started off scheme after scheme in my aching head for the downfall of Al Rachell. They raced through my mind in a savoury mist of mulligan and beans slowly heating up on the stove.

At last I called out to him.

'You going to let me have some of that grub?'

He didn't answer at once, maybe just because he wanted to torture me. Rachell was the kind that liked hurting folks.

121

'Lew didn't say nothin' about givin' you grub.'

'Ah, come on, Al,' I said. 'If you eat all that you're cookin' you'll swell up like one of those new-fangled balloons and burst.' This didn't seem to please him much for he came over and gave me another kick in the ribs, a bit harder this time.

'You shut yore trap, mister, or I'll shut it for keeps.'

I looked up into the huge sullen stupid face and I knew I'd have to be a damn sight smarter than I'd ever been before if I was going to get away from Al Rachell. First off I'd got to get rid of whatever was tying my wrists behind my back.

I could hear him moving around again and making noises as if he was piling up a plate. I heard him coming towards me. He bent down and pulled me up into a sitting position with my back to a wall. Then he sat down at the table about six feet away with a big plate and a spoon. He proceeded to fill this with stew and beans for the next five minutes while I watched and saliva collected in my mouth until I wanted to be sick.

Rachell got up at once and went over to a cupboard. He came back with a jug of what was probably whisky. He tipped this up several times gurgling with pleasure as the raw spirit ran down his throat. When he'd done drinking he sat for a bit looking like a contented ape. I tried again. 'How about some of that grub?' I said. Surprisingly he stood up and went over to the stove.

'Lew said to keep you alive,' he muttered over his shoulder. He filled a plate and brought it over to the table. Then he pulled his six-gun and laid it carefully on the table a couple of feet from the plate. I could almost hear his small cunning mind ticking over as he made his preparations. When he had things as he wanted them he came over to me and picked me up like a sack of beans and carted me over to the table. He threw me into a chair and proceeded to unloose the rope round my wrists.

'One wrong move outa you,' he growled.

'An' I'll gun you down where you sit.'

The rope was off and I took time rubbing my wrists till the blood flowed again and some life came back into them. He pushed the plate of food towards me and sat down on the other side of the table with the big Colt close to his right hand.

I started to eat, still trying to work out a trick that would faze Rachell. What I needed was something big enough and hard enough to hit him with if I could get within hitting distance. The whisky jug was on the table and as I chewed on the none-too-tender meat in the mulligan he drew it towards him, paused and looked at me. He figured I might jump him maybe while he was lifting the jug.

'Salud,' I said, raising a spoonful of beans.

He made no reply, but raised the jug slowly, his eyes watching me closely over the mouth of it. I was tempted but I figured it was wiser to wait. Al Rachell was not the kind to go to the well once only. He'd drink again and maybe again and when he'd lost some of his caution I'd choose my own time and my own weapon.

He lowered the jug, smacking his lips with pleasure and greed. I picked up two beans on my spoon and ate them slowly. If I finished too soon he'd have the rope back on me and my chance would be gone. He was lifting the jug again and letting the whisky gurgle down his throat. A trickle of it ran down the left side of his chin and dripped on to his vest. The jug came down on the table-top with a bit of a thud. Hands losing control, I thought. He stared at me with his small pig-like eyes. Just below his nose a wart with hairs growing out of it stood out like some badge of infamy.

'Ain't told you about what happened back in '66,' he said. The words were faintly blurred. 'Hev I?'

'You ain't told me,' I said.

'We was up in the Bitterroots, me an' another.' He gave me a leery look and I just nodded.

'We was huntin' an' a norther came down

on us sudden. We holed up in a cave just below timber-line. We were short on grub and after three days in the cave it gave out. We couldn't move. The snow was fifteen foot deep all around.' He stared at me with his small red eyes. 'We jes' couldn't git out.'

'What saved you?' A faint curiosity was stirring in me.

'The other one died,' he said. 'That's how I kept myself alive.'

I might have guessed from just looking at him, at the big hulk of his body, the loose, fleshy mouth and the animal eyes still peering at me from under the thick, bushy brows.

He was peering out all right from the cave in which he'd live for as long as there was breath in this hideous body. But his mind was far away in another cave and maybe to forget it he raised the jug once more and drank.

It was the moment. I rose, reached across and jammed the mouth of the jug as far down his throat as I could. I brought the table over on top of him and jumped wide to get my hands on a weapon. The nearest was a poker standing near the stove. I grabbed it and turning saw him rising up to come at me. He did in a clumsy rush. I stepped aside, put out a foot and tripped him up. He fell with a crash against a low cupboard. There wasn't time to get at him with the poker. He was up, snarling and grunting. He moved towards me with his big arms stretched wide. I dodged round the upturned table and he stopped, glaring at me across the legs of the table.

'Stand an' fight,' he growled.

'The odds ain't equal,' I said.

He came at me again, right over the table. He caught a foot in it and came down flat, but not before one of his great fists swung against the side of my head. It felt like the head of a lumberjack's axe. I went over like a ninepin, rolled and swayed to my feet. He was up again, mad as a bear and just as dangerous. He rushed with his head down. Again I side-stepped but this time I managed to lay the poker with all the strength I had on the back of his neck. He fell flat on his face, motionless.

I kept well out of reach. Al Rachell could be playing possum. I waited. No sound, no movement. I suddenly felt sick. Sick and old and dirty. My head throbbed like a tired old engine. I looked around expecting to see the bodies of Ep Cartledge and Dan. They weren't there. I took a shaky pasear to the door and went out into the air. It felt good after the inside of what had once been the Cartledge home.

I went back inside. I wanted my hat, my gun too, if it was still there. Rachell lay where he'd fallen. Still no sound, no movement. I suddenly realised that he was probably dead. I went across and heaved him over. One look was enough. Al Rachell would trouble the world no more. I looked around for my gun and found it on top of a cupboard. My hat was lying in a corner.

Out in the sunshine it was warm and peaceful. Two new-turned mounds of earth stuck up in the grass a little distance from the house. It was as I stood there that one of those things you read of in story books and only half believe happened to me. For some reason or other I suddenly gave the whistle I'd used for a couple of years to call Bessie, my mare. I wasn't expecting anything at all. I'd just done it out of habit and suddenly out of the cottonwoods she came a-trotting towards me. As she drew near she threw up her head and whinnied with what I assumed was pleasure. I figured it wouldn't be half as much as I felt. Well, we went through the usual motions of greeting and then I ambled across to what was left of the barn to look for a saddle. It was all pretty badly burnt but my saddle was still there along with a couple of others that had escaped the flames. I lifted it and then saddled up. There was nothing to be done at the Cartledge house so I climbed on to Bessie and rode away.

We trotted easily and comfortably east towards the Basin and then I reined in. We were on the crest of the last ridge looking down. It was time for a little plain and fancy thinking and my head had just about recovered from the clumping Rachell had given it, not to mention the gun-barrel swipe that had put me to sleep the night before. I looked out towards the long brown-yellow sweep of the valley and the blue hills in the far distance. It was the kind of thing I enjoyed looking at. I could ride across those Basin lands and up into the far blue hills and be rid of all the ruckus of the Urquharts and the townsfolk and the homesteaders and the outlaws like buzzards, only worse. There's a time for a man to ride on all right. And maybe this was it. It wouldn't be the first time I'd ridden on. I'd ridden away from trouble down in Arizona and Texas. Maybe it was a habit. I sat there brooding on what lay before me and into my mind came pictures of young Dan and old Cartledge being shot in the back and Mrs Cartledge wailing over the body of her dead husband. No, I figured, the time to ride on has passed. There was Lew Owens and Sam Point and others. For some reason or other I had to do something about them.

I said 'Giddup' to Bessie and we rode downgrade to the valley bottom and across it in the general direction of the Urquhart ranch. It was there that the next trouble would boil up and the more I thought about it the less I liked the idea of Sarah Urquhart being mixed up with folk like Owens and the rest of them. Even as I thought of it a shiver crawled down my spine. Someone walking over your grave as my old Ma used to say. But it could be someone else's, someone who mattered.

I rode on and suddenly I began to feel sick. My eyes felt like two small balls of lead and my stomach seemed like it was living a life of its own. We went on and on and the heat of the afternoon sun lay like a hot load on my back. I gritted my teeth and hung on to Bessie but not for long. Suddenly the sky tilted and I knew I was falling. Then I didn't know any more.

When I came to there was something

against my mouth and a shadow between me and the light. I tried to get up and a voice said:

'You'll only upset it, Mr Ross.'

It was a woman's voice and I reckoned I could give a name to it. After all, women in the territory of Wyoming were about as scarce as bears in Boston. I wasn't likely to be far wrong when I said:

'Well, doggone it, if it ain't Miss Urquhart herself.'

I pulled myself up as I spoke, shook my head a bit and took another look around. My eyes came to rest on the same trim figure I'd first met up with on the rimrock with a Winchester in its arms.

'Yes, doggone it, it's Miss Urquhart her very own self and plumb lucky for you I happened along this way.' Listening I realized she'd changed her manner of speaking and then hot on the heels of the first thought came a second. She was giving a pretty fair imitation of the way Johnny Ross would talk. I just sat there giving her a

132

cold mean look and she sat back on her heels and looked at me with just as much coldness and meanness as I was giving her. I couldn't help noticing that, however she might be looking at me, she was a mighty handsome sight sitting there with a little hard-crowned stetson on the back of her curly head, a dark blue wool shirt open at the neck and the rest of her encased in a pair of old faded tight levis tucked into short, high-heeled riding-boots. Yessirree, she sure was a comely sight.

She must have become aware of my appraising eye because she blushed and then to cover it, said nastily: 'Been killing any more men lately, Mr Ross?'

'None,' I said shortly, and then remembering Al Rachell, 'I mean, Yup.'

'Which probably goes some way to explaining the terrible mess you're in,' she said.

'Yup,' I said, not being in any mood for overlong conversations right then. I hurled myself to my feet, slow and easy, but even then when I was up I lurched forward and would have flopped down again if she hadn't grabbed me and held on.

'Look,' she said severely. 'You're in no state to go wandering off by yourself. You're coming back to the ranch with me and we'll patch you up.'

'Yes'm,' I said, meekly, and allowed myself to be led to where old Bessie was standing hipshot and tired of swishing her tail. Miss Urquhart helped me up. Then she went over to her pony and climbed into the saddle.

We rode off and reached the ranch just as blue dusk was beginning to fold down over the rangeland. We went in and she made me sit in a rocker in the big old kitchen. Then she got water and a cloth and bathed the big bruise and cut on the back of my head.

'It's a beauty,' she said, kind of pleased. 'Big as an egg.'

'Feels like I'd grown an extra head,' I mumbled.

She finished cleaning me up and put nice cool stuff on the lump and I began to feel fine.

'Now you sit there while I get some food,' she said, briskly. I didn't say anything. It sure was good just to sit and watch her wielding two frying-pans into which she put steak and eggs and onions. It didn't take long. She sat down at a table with me and we tucked into the food like two half-starved bears after a long winter.

When we got to the cigarette-rolling stage I asked her the question that had been worrying around in me ever since we'd set foot in the Urquhart ranch.

'Where's everybody gone?'

'They're all out rounding up the cattle,' she said.

'That's a bit sudden,' I said. 'And come to think of it a bit unusual this late in the year.'

She gave me a long, slow, measuring look. Almost as if she was making up her mind about me.

'I reckon I can trust you, Johnny Ross,' she said at last. 'Jess Antrim has taken over since my Dad died. He tells me now what we should do. He decided that the best thing for us would be to gather in the cattle fast and sell.'

'I don't see why,' I said.

'He thinks the outlaws are in cahoots with the Cartledges and that soon they'll be too strong for us. By spring, he says, we'll have no cattle left. So the round-up is on.'

'It sure is,' said a voice from behind us. We turned. It was Jess Antrim giving us a cold blue eye. He must have come in from the front of the house and mighty quickly at that.

'Howsomever,' he continued, 'I don't see what business it is of yours, mister.'

And he gave me the full blue glare I'd seen before. He was a small hot-tempered man and yet there was something about him I figured I could trust.

'I didn't say it was any of my business. I just happened along and Miss Urquhart here was explaining where everybody had gone.'

'Mighty nice and sociable of Miss Urqu-hart, I'm sure,' he sneered.

'That will do, Jess Antrim,' said the girl. 'You may be helping to run this ranch, but you are only helping.'

'Yes'm,' he said, quiet-like, no louder than the rattle of a sidewinder.

'Something quite other is my business,' I said. 'And that's the part you played in the attack on the Cartledge's house last night.'

I felt rather than saw Sarah Urquhart react to that one. Antrim's eyes slitted and he made no reply, so I went on.

'There wasn't much left of the Cartledge place or the Cartledge family by the time you and your roughnecks had finished with it, just one poor woman with her husband and her son dead, and not much left to live for.'

'Is all this true, Johnny Ross?' Her voice was quiet and humble-like.

'I was there. That's how I came by this lump on my head.'

There was a moment's silence while they took in what I said. I looked at Sarah Urquhart and was sure surprised to see the change in her. She looked madder than seven hundred hornets but it was worse than that. Behind the anger there was a grief and when she spoke it was quietly.

'I shan't be needing your help any more, Jess Antrim. You can pack your bags and go.'

'Go where?'

'Anywhere you like,' she replied. 'So long as it's far away from here.'

'I've worked with your Pa for close on ten years now and all you can do is just give me my time like I was some fiddle-footed cowhand.'

'I've had enough of feuding and fighting,' she said. 'You'll have to find work some-where else.'

'I doubt you'll be able to do that for some time to come,' I put in. 'When you've packed your bag you're coming along of me.'

'Where?'

'To the calaboose in Pitchfork. I'm taking you in for being concerned in the murder of Dan Cartledge. Someone's got to pay for what happened up there last night.'

Now I should have known that Jess Antrim was not the kind of hombre to let himself be arrested peaceful-like but not being well versed in the ways of lawmen and such I just left myself wide open to trouble. I should have drawn on him while I had the advantage. As it was, he whipped out his Colt just as I finished speaking.

'I ain't goin' nowhere with you, mister,' he said grimly. 'I've got a job to attend to and neither you nor this little lady hyar is a-goin' to get in my way.'

He paused, and faintly into the deadly quiet of the room came the sound of a horse's hooves growing louder and louder as the rider brought it into the yard. There was a moment's silence during which we watched each other with loving care and then the door burst open and a rider, young, red-faced and sweating, appeared. He stared at our little tableau for a breathless pause, then blurted out:

'The cattle, Jess, the cattle.'

'Yeah?'

'They've took the lot. They've killed two of the crew, Matt an' Pete.'

'I'm comin',' said Antrim. He turned to me and gestured with his Colt.

'Go get this ranny's gun, kid, an' watch him.'

The young rider circled round behind me and lifted my gun carefully out of its holster.

'Shuck the slugs out of it an' give it back,' said Antrim. The rider did as he was bid.

'We're goin' now,' said Antrim. 'It might be a good idea to stay where you are until we're out of sight.'

'Don't think you'll get away,' I said. 'I'll ride you down yet.'

He gave me a long slow scrutiny before answering. 'Yeah,' he said, 'I reckon you will.' Then he stepped out through the door and slammed it behind him.

CHAPTER SEVEN

There wasn't much I could do about Jess Antrim so I waited until he and the other Urquhart rider were well under way. I looked at Miss Urquhart and realised how hard she'd been hit by what had come out about the Cartledges. She had sat down in a rocker and was crying a little. This worried me no end because I've had mighty little experience of women's tears, and wasn't at all sure what to do about it.

'Reckon I'll ride around a bit, Miss Urquhart,' I said at last. 'Someone had better look into what's going on. If anyone's rustlin' your cattle then they've got to be stopped.'

'I'd be grateful if you could do something,' she said, softly.

'Then I'll be on my way,' I said. I picked up my hat and walked over to the door. I turned half-round when I reached it.

'It was mighty kind of you to bring me here and tend to my hurts,' I said, awkwardly.

'I couldn't very well leave you out on the range in the state you were in,' she said, regaining something of her normal way of looking at things.

'No, ma'am,' I said. 'Especially when it was a fine handsome little feller like me.'

'I hadn't noticed any of the things you mention other than the "little" part of it,' she replied tartly.

Well that's put the cap on it as it were and I opened the door to get out before we exchanged any more salty remarks.

'Hope you can manage to climb on to that old jughead of yours,' she called out sweetly. My only answer was a very poor one. I slammed the door behind me and made my way to where Bessie was waiting for me. At that moment I was prepared to swear that there was a lot more to be said for a mare than for any woman I'd ever met up with.

My next move had to be a careful one.

There wasn't much sense in getting tangled up with Jess Antrim and the Circle U riders and, if their cattle were getting rustled, then they wouldn't stop to ask questions if they ran into me. They'd either string me up or shoot me down and high game or low game had mighty little appeal to Johnny Ross.

It was a fine clear night out in the yard, all silver spaces and black shadows from the full moon riding high, wide and handsome above me. I left the main trail leading out of the ranch as soon as we cleared the fence and cut over to the west. I was soon up on the flank of a long low ridge with what looked like flat grazing land stretching out eastwards into empty moonlit space. The trail I was on led downgrade after a couple of miles and before getting down on to the flat I had my long cagey look at the land. The full moonlight made shadows here and there and as my old Ma used to say, 'It's better to be safe than sorry.'

I rode on into the flat wide valley, crossed it seeing nothing and let Bessie take her time as we began to climb again. There were trees on this side and once, suddenly, out of a clump over to my right an owl hooted and I tensed. But it was only an owl. We reached the flat top of the table-land. From here I could begin a sweep that would take me north and then east of the Urquhart place. Somewhere inside the circle I was drawing would be the rustlers, the cattle and Jess Antrim's riders. How I was going to sit in on the game I didn't know. There were three things I wanted, Urquhart's murderer, Dan Cartledge's murderer and Sarah Urquhart's cattle. I'd take the latter back, set 'em down in her backyard and then walk out on her once and for all.

I rode on, changing course by the stars. North by north-east and the terrain was changing again. Many more trees and a trail leading round rimrock with another broad valley below. I was getting mighty tired so I halted Bessie and climbed heavily out of the saddle. If I didn't hit the sack soon something would hit me. I ground-haltered

Bessie and fed her some oats. Then I took my blanket and rolled myself in it and went to sleep as fast as a jack-rabbit heading for home.

I woke in the thin light of dawn, stiff and cold and hungry. Bessie greeted me with a snort and I started to light a small twig fire. When I had it going I stuck a coffee pot on it. Then I gave Bessie a rub down and the rest of the oats I had with me. I fried some bacon, ate it and poured some hot black coffee on top of it. By the time I had smoked a cigarette it was full day and we were all set to go.

I rolled up my few belongings, saddled Bessie and climbed aboard. She crowhopped sedately just to show that she was as good as ever and off we went at a gentle trot. It was time we got down to cases, I figured. After all we weren't riding around Wyoming territory for our health. If we turned east I reckoned we ought to make contact with someone soon.

We went on quietly eastwards and had

reached the western side of a canyon when at last things began to happen. First of all a couple of gunshots that echoed up out of the valley depths and sent some birds whirling up into the air. I reined in and listened. There was another noise now, growing with every ticking second. A deep-seated rumbling roar. I knew it like all men who have lived in the West. It was the roar of cattle stampeding, thousands of hooves beating their fear into the dust of a trail, as uncontrollable as a river that's burst its banks.

I put Bessie's head down-trail towards the valley bottom and halted her again as the picture unfolded itself before me. They were spread out before and below me, a great brown liquid carpet. And at its edges there were the small mounted figures of riders. There was something else, something you don't see or anyways something I'd never seen before. There were a dozen riders spread out below me right in the path of the stampeding cattle now no more than fifty yards away from them. And as I watched they let go with their guns plumb into the faces of the cows coming at them. Some of them went down. Some turned off and beat their way up the valley slopes. But the pressure from behind was too great. The great brown mass roared on and the riders wheeled their mounts to get away. Some did. I saw two go down and disappear under the swirling heaving mass of fear-crazed steers. There were more shots and I saw two bunches of riders come together on the edge of the stampede. More shots and a horse went high up on its hind legs and then let out the high shrill cry of animal fear.

And then the last of the running cattle were past and gone. In their wake there was nothing now but the trampled grass and the carcasses of dead steers and three other shapes that didn't look like the shapes of animals. Then the riders suddenly broke up into two quite separate groups. I heard a thin high yell come up from one of them and then suddenly they hightailed it after the cattle. The ones who were left stood around for a few minutes and then they too broke up. Three of them rode away east across the valley and up the slope on the side away from me. One went on up the valley in the direction of the stampede and one rode slowly towards where I was sheltering by a thorn-bush.

I watched him come up the trail, a thin hunched figure on a tired claybank. He got nearer. I judged he'd be one of the Urquhart hands from his looks and his clothes, just a young puncher who'd had enough of other folks' quarrels and was on his way out. It wouldn't do to let him get too near in the state he was in. He'd probably start shooting almost before I'd got my mouth open. So I sung out when he was still more than fifty yards away.

'Don't start pullin' your gun and blazin' away when you hear me,' I shouted. 'I've nothing agin you and aim to do nothin' more than say "Howdy" and ride on.'

I watched him as I spoke and all he did was to ride straight on towards me without any sign that he'd even heard me. However he reined in as he rode up and gave me a long careful look. He was young, unshaven and dead-beat but his eyes were clear and honest.

'You one of them?'

'Depends who you mean by "them",' I said and to ease the situation I crooked my left leg round the saddlehorn and began to roll myself a smoke.

'One of them goddam son-of-a-bitch rustlers,' he said.

'I've been a lot of things in my time, mister,' I replied, 'but I've never been a rustler. I'm Johnny Ross.'

His tired eyes must have seized on my badge at long last.

'If you're a sheriff,' he said, 'you'd better git goin' after the gang that pinched our herd. I'm Wes Bevin.'

'Maybe you would bring me up to date on what's goin' on,' I said. 'I'm just a mite fazed right now.'

He climbed slowly and wearily off his

cayuse and I did the same. I pulled out the makings and offered them to him. He began to roll a cigarette and said nothing until he'd finished it and lit it.

'The whole thing was mighty sudden,' he began. 'It started last night when there was only two riders watching the herd.'

'Where was this?'

'About ten miles south of where we are now,' he said. 'They jumped us in the half-light and took the cattle right from under our noses. Gil Walters got tromped when they ran and Pete Soames got a slug through his leg. We sent someone to fetch Jess Antrim and when he got over to us we trailed the herd to where the rustlers had bedded it down for the night. There wasn't much we could do 'cept wait for morning. Then we cut up in front of them thinking we could stop 'em in the canyon. They must have figured we'd do that so they just stampeded the herd. The rest you know, stranger.'

'Yup,' I said. 'The rest I know. But I'd like to know what's going to happen next.'

He stared at me dully for a moment without replying. He dropped his cigarette butt on the ground and rubbed it out with his boot-heel.

'Nothin's going to happen next,' he said. 'The Circle U's all washed up. There's nothin' left. I'm ridin' on.'

'Where?'

'Anywhere I can find a job and don't have to reach for my gun every time a shadow moves.'

'And what's to happen to Miss Urquhart and her cattle? Or don't you care? Or maybe you're just plumb scairt.'

His pale face flushed a dull red.

'I ain't scairt, mister. But one agin a dozen or more – no, sirree! That's not Wes Bevin's idea of fair play.'

I turned away from him. There wasn't anything more to say. I didn't reckon he was being any more than commonsensical, though I wasn't going to say so to his face.

I climbed up on to Bessie.

Hasta la vista, I said. 'I'll go to see

whether there's anything I can save from the ruins.'

I rode off down into the valley. There were a few dead steers lying around and then I came to a body lying crumpled up on the grass. I dismounted and went over to it. He was face down but I knew before I turned him over and looked into the sightless blue eyes staring emptily up into the sky that it was Jess Antrim. He'd been shot once right through the chest and must have died instanter.

I left him and rode over to look at two other bodies. I had seen one of them when the Circle U crew had come to Pitchfork. The other I didn't know. Both of them had been tromped to death by the stampeding steers. Twenty-five years old, give or take a year or so, and nothing to show but a few fancy duds, a gunbelt and a gun and now lying dead on the trampled grass. A hard, tough, ugly world with mighty little to show of the frills, the glamour, the excitement that Easterners pictured when they talked about cowboys or the far-flung western frontier.

I was wakened by the sound of a horse approaching. I turned and saw Wes Bevin coming slowly towards me. I wasn't surprised. He hadn't looked the kind that rode away and left a woman like Sarah Urquhart in trouble.

'Can't leave 'em lying around for the coyotes to get at,' he said, pulling up alongside of where I was standing near the dead man.

'Nope,' I said. 'It would seem kinda heartless.'

'We'll need a spade,' he said. 'I'll ride over to the spread and get one. It ain't more'n an hour's ride from hyar.'

There wasn't anything else we could do so we said '*Adiós*,' and off he cantered.

Well I did my usual little spell of plain an' fancy thinking but got no further forward than being surprised at finding myself trailing along behind a gang of rustlers and a herd of stolen beef, with a tin star on my vest and a kind of hankering for something.

Every now and then I found myself thinking of Sarah Urquhart. I rolled a cigarette and thought about her some more. Not in any particular way, you'll understand. I just had a sort of picture in my mind and every now and then as I said I took a peek at it. Well this went on for some time and I rolled another cigarette and found myself a nice warm place just off the main trail with a cottonwood tree to rest my back against. Once and then again my eyes began to close and I'd snap back to wakefulness but they seemed to close again and I slept.

I woke suddenly some time later and could tell by the sun that quite a spell of time had slid by. More than a couple of hours, which was all Wes Bevin would have needed to get to the ranch and back. I looked at my watch and went hot and then cold. It was more than four hours since Wes Bevin had left me. Something was badly wrong and I figured I'd better find out pronto.

Maybe he'd decided to ride on after all, I thought, as I saddled up Bessie and then mounted. Maybe she made him stay for some grub before letting him come back with the spade. Maybe. Maybe. A dozen or more possibles came to me as I rode back the way I'd come. But the nearer I got to the Urquhart place the more troubled I became.

I reached it at last and everything was very quiet. I rode into the yard. No sign of Miss Sarah Urquhart or Wes Bevin or any other human being.

I called out, 'Hallo, the house!'

Nothing at all. Everything there, the empty yard, the long, low, frame house drowsed in the late afternoon sunlight. But there was nothing calm and peaceful about the scene. It was all bad and tensed up. I'd seen places like it before in the war days back in '64. Houses into which death had come and where death remained like a dark shadow skulking in a corner.

I got down off Bessie and tied her reins to a post. Slowly I walked back towards the porch and with every step my fears of what lay inside increased. I went up the two steps.

Sweat gathered on my forehead and ran down into my eyes. I wiped it away, aware as I did so that I had drawn my gun without knowing. I reached the door and froze. There was someone inside. Someone who had given a low half-strangled cry of pain. I kicked the door open and ran in, my gun at the ready. I jumped over to the left as I entered and immediately fell headlong over something on the floor.

I lay there, with the breath knocked out of me for a long minute. Then slowly I got to my feet. There was someone lying between me and the door and he groaned again as I moved towards him. The light wasn't good but it was just enough for me to know that it was Wes Bevin stretched out there.

I turned and went over to the table on which an oil-lamp stood. I managed to get it lit and then I went back to Wes Bevin. I put the lamp on the floor near his head and had a look at him. He'd been plugged, once so far as I could tell through the left shoulder. There was blood in a pool under him and a great dark stain on his vest and shirt. His eyes were shut and he was breathing badly. I took out my knife and slit his shirt open and had a look at the wound. It was pretty nasty looking. I felt around at the back but the bullet hadn't come through so this was a job for the local sawbones if I could get to him in time. There was only one hope for Wes Bevin and that was to get him back to Pitchfork as quickly as possible. There was something else I had to know before we left the ranch. Where was Sarah Urquhart?

I stood up and had a look round the big living-room. I could see a kind of sideboard across the room. Maybe there'd be some there. I went across and opened the doors. It was there all right – a bottle of Old Crow and hardly touched. I found a glass and half-filled it. Then I carried it back and propping Wes Bevin up with one hand I fed him whisky with the other. It had the effect I aimed at. He spluttered a bit, coughed and then opened his eyes.

'Wha-a-t?' he croaked.

I said, 'Have another jolt of red-eye and then we'll talk.'

He managed to get a little more inside him.

'Where's Miss Sarah?' I said when I thought he was sufficiently awake.

'Miss Sarah! Miss Sarah.' His eyes rolled wild and I thought he was going to pass out again. But he held on. And slowly I got the information I wanted.

'Three of 'em hyar when I rode in. They had Miss Sarah hawg-tied and ready to leave.' He paused and sighed. 'Don't ask me why, mister. I jest don't know the answer.'

'How did you get the slug in you?'

'I said...' His voice trailed off for a moment but it came back. 'I said to leave her be. They laughed. One of 'em said they aimed to make her write her will an' sign it and then they'd leave her be. I tried to get out my gun. It wasn't no use. One of 'em, the small one, gunned me down before I'd even cleared leather.'

He sighed again and his eyes closed. Then

they opened again.

'They've taken off somewhere. You go and get her back, Mr Ross.'

'Yes,' I said. 'I'll get her back but first we'll get you to a doc. Then we'll see about Miss Sarah.'

I knew it was less'n useless to take off alone after the men who'd got Sarah Urquhart. And anyways I couldn't leave Wes Bevin to die slow but sure in the empty ranch house. I figured there'd be a flat-bed wagon around some place and with this I could get him into town to a doc and then see about rallying some of the good towns-folk to my aid. Yessir, that's what I thought, but as some poet once said, according to my Ma, 'the plans of mice and men sure have a way of coming unstuck.'

CHAPTER EIGHT

I found a flat-bed wagon as I expected out in the big barn. I hitched Wes Bevin's claybank and old Bessie to it and drove it around to the front door. Somehow or other, seeing that he was a good forty pounds heavier than I am, I managed to get him out of the ranch-house and into the wagon. Then I fetched the saddles and put them in too. There wasn't any more I could do so I climbed up on to the seat, shook out the reins and got the horses on the move.

It was all of fifteen miles to Pitchfork but it seemed like a hundred for my mind wouldn't leave go of the thought of Sarah Urquhart in the hands of hombres like Lew Owens, Jake Gillams or Sam Point. It was only a crumb of comfort to remember that Al Rachell was dead. Thought after thought chased themselves round and round in my head and the more I thought the more scared I got. By the time we reached the outskirts of town I was in a muck sweat of anxiety.

We drew in and as usual the place almost seemed empty. If ever there was a town that breathed out unwelcome and a kind of fear it was this one. I pulled in outside the shack they'd given me as a Marshal's office. Then I thought I'd be more likely to find someone at The Cattleman's House. So I drove on and halted at the bottom of the steps leading to the saloon doors.

I climbed down and went in. The barman was there setting things up for the evening's social business. In the far corner of the long room two men were sitting at a table. They had a whisky bottle and a deck of cards. The barman saw me and sang out, 'Howdy, Mr Ross!'

There wasn't time for social chit-chat.

'You seen Roselaw?' I said. 'Or any other pillars of this community?'

162

'Mr Roselaw's over to Mike Channings,' he said kind of stiffly.

'Go and get 'em,' I said. 'Tell 'em hell's broke loose over at the Urquhart spread an' I need help.'

He stood there with his mouth hanging open like a dead fish.

'Goddammit,' I shouted. 'Ain't you got ears? Go get Roselaw, Channing and anyone else you can find.'

'Yessir, Mr Ross,' he sang out and trotted round the bar and out through the bat-wings.

I stood there, tried to roll myself a cigarette, made a mess of it and threw the wreckage on to the floor. Then the barman came running back.

'They're on their way,' he said.

'Right. You come help me with a wounded man I've got out in the street.'

I turned and we went out to the wagon. Wes Bevin was awake but his eyes were too bright and his cheeks were too red. Between us we got him out of the wagon, up the steps and into the saloon. Then we moved up-stairs and into a bedroom. We put him down on the bed. It was beginning to get dark so I lit the oil-lamp. Downstairs there was the sound of men tramping into the saloon. So I went to the head of the stairs and called out: 'Come on up. I've got a wounded man up hyar.'

They came up in a solemn file, Roselaw, Channing, Ed Morgan and a small pot-bellied hombre I'd never seen before.

'This is Doc Hassens,' said Roselaw.

The doc came over to look at Wes Bevin. Someone held the oil-lamp close and he probed around, humming and hawing until at last he seemed satisfied.

'Not so bad as it looks,' he said. 'The bullet's buried in the fleshy part of his shoulder. I'll have to operate.'

He went off at once to get his tools.

'How did this happen?' said Ed Morgan, looking at me.

'It's a long story,' I said. 'But the nub of it's this. The Urquhart cattle have been rustled, the crew's broken apart at the seams and disappeared an' Miss Urquhart's been kidnapped.'

'Miss Urquhart,' said Channing incredulously. 'Who by?'

'By the same gang that stole the cattle an' put a slug into Wes Bevin here.'

'That'd be Sam Point and the crew he's been running with. They was sidin' the Cartledge family before ... before...' Morgan's voice suddenly petered out.

'Before Ep Cartledge and his son were murdered.' I finished the sentence for him. 'Where's Mrs Cartledge now?'

'She's staying with Mrs Brill,' said Morgan. 'The Brills were friends of the Cartledges, sided them over this trouble with the Urquharts.'

I remembered Joshua Brill coming in on the night I'd first gone to the Cartledge home. She'd be all right with them, so far as she'd ever be all right again.

There was a sound of feet on the stairs and back came Doc Hassens. He had a little black bag out of which he produced some mighty dangerous-looking implements, a small bottle and a sponge.

'Just a sniff of this,' he said, pouring from the bottle on to the sponge, 'and we'll have no difficulty at all.' He placed the sponge over Bevin's nose. 'No difficulty at all.' When he seemed satisfied he had me remove Bevin's shirt and then he got to work. In less than five minutes he had yanked out the slug, staunched the blood and was binding up the wound.

'He'll feel a bit groggy when he wakes,' he said as he packed his bag. 'But he'll be as fit as a fiddle in a few hours' time.'

There wasn't anything else we could do so we all trooped downstairs to the bar where we found Joe Humphress and Gabbit, the liveryman, and we all had a snort together to celebrate the successful operation. But as I drank my second dose of red-eye I knew it was time to come to the point. I wanted help and these were the only people who could give it to me. I couldn't ride alone over to wherever Lew Owens and his gang had got Sarah Urquhart. I've done some stupid things in my time but I wasn't so stupid as to think I could ride into the rustlers hide-out, pick up Sarah Urquhart and walk out with her and a whole skin.

They were all standing around the bar smiling and talking a blue streak about things when I put in my two-bit fire-cracker.

'Jest before the Doc got to work on Wes Bevin,' I said during a short lull in the chatter, 'I told you gents that Miss Urquhart had been kidnapped by Lew Owens and his long-riding pals. I figure we'd better have a little pow-wow about that right now.'

There was a silence you could have cut with a bowie-knife. At last, Humphress said, 'Well, this is a terrible situation.'

'Yes, indeed, indeed,' said Ed Morgan, staring intent-like up at the ceiling.

'Is it possible now that you have made a mistake, Mr Ross?' put in Roselaw. His eyes were dark with disbelief or something I didn't savvy. Not then.

'No,' I said. 'There's no mistake. Wes Bevin was shot down a-tryin' to stop 'em doing it. They've got her all right and we've got to get her back.'

'Yes,' said Ed Morgan. 'Yes, of course.' His face was all crinkled up with the strain of trying to cope with the situation.

'What do you want us to do?' said Roselaw trying to look business-like and rarin' to go.

'Do?' I said. 'There's only one thing we can do and that's assemble a posse and ride out after her pronto.'

There was another thick silence but longer than before.

'Well,' I said, after what seemed like an hour, 'who's ready to be deputized? Step up and take the oath.'

'Look, Mr Ross,' said Humphress at last. 'It's no good asking us to make a posse. We're just ordinary folks. We've got businesses to look after. We don't know horses an' we don't know guns. We wouldn't be any help, now would we?' He looked round at the others and they all nodded agreement like a lot of Chinamen, at a prayer-meeting.

'You all lent a hand or rather a gun when the Urquhart crew was in town,' I pointed out. 'Why not now?'

'They was in town,' said Gabbit, speaking for the first time. His long black moustaches drooped gloomily around his mouth. 'We can't leave our town. It ain't nacheral.'

'The Urquharts never did raise a hand to help us,' said Humphress. 'Why should we help them now?'

'It isn't *them*,' I said slow and careful. 'It's *her*. It's one young innocent girl in the hands of a gang of desperadoes.'

'Innocent? That's as maybe.' It was Rose-law, his face gone slack and ugly with a sneer of unbelief. I swung at him with my left and hit him good and true on his twisted mouth. He went over like a skittle. Two of them grabbed me and Roselaw scrambled to his feet.

'Now, gentlemen, now,' said Ed Morgan. 'Quarrelling won't help. I suggest we go away and talk about this for a while. Then we'll come back with a plan which we'll put to Marshal Ross. Agreed?'

They all seemed to agree and drifted off, some place else, with Roselaw applying a handkerchief to his bruised lips.

I stood there for a few moments too riled to move or think.

'I figure another drink might help,' said a voice behind me. It was the bartender.

I turned and looked at him without affection. I just didn't like the inhabitants of Pitchfork. I nodded, not trusting my voice and he pushed a bottle and a shot-glass towards me.

'What's wrong with folks in this town?' I said at last.

'They're just folks.' He avoided my eye and rubbed the well-polished bar-top vigorously.

'They're scairt, right down to their boot-heels,' I said.

'Mebbe, Mister Ross,' he said. Then suddenly he leaned right across the bar until his face was no more than an inch from mine. 'They're scairt of curly wolves like the two in the corner. They're scairt of the men up in the hills. They're scairt of their own shadows.'

I remembered the two hombres who'd been sitting in the corner when I'd first arrived with Wes Bevin.

'Yes,' I said. 'I reckon I know what you mean.'

'Ain't said so much in a coon's age,' said the bartender taking up a glass and giving it a shine.

'You figurin' to eat here tonight?' he asked.

'Yeah,' I said. 'Right now. I'll need a full stomach to face what lies ahead.'

'Right,' he said. 'Be with you in fifteen minutes.' He went towards the kitchen.

I rolled and lit a cigarette, filled the shot-glass again and began to feel better. I took a quick look at the pair still sitting at their table in the corner of the saloon. They didn't look much like curly wolves, just nondescript riders, one bearded and rather fat, the other thinner and clean-shaven. And then I noticed that the one nearest to me was wearing a gun low down on his left leg, with the holster tied down into a leather thong. They could be a couple of grub-line riders, drifters, saddle-tramps. Maybe I'd better keep an eye open on their movements. My cigarette burned down to a stub. I finished my drink. Then the bartender returned, laid a table near the bar, shot out again and came back with a large plate of steak, eggs and potatoes. I sat down and pitched in. I was hungry and not at all sure when I'd eat again. The food was good and I ate till I could eat no more. The bartender brought a big mug of coffee and I poured it on top of the steak to keep it company. It was time for the local citizens to have made up their minds but they didn't seem to be in any hurry. I was.

I stood up and went to the bar. The barman looked worried. Maybe I had that effect on him.

I said, 'Look, I can't wait around here much longer. Go and tell the boys in the back room that I want an answer – pronto!'

He came around the bar obediently and trotted off through the door which the citizens of Pitchfork had used. There was a moment's heavy silence broken only by the sound of a horse trotting by in the street outside. Then the door opened again and they all filed in. They looked a little flat, a little shame-faced and they swaggered a little to hide their shame.

They came up to where I stood and I knew exactly what they were going to say. I just wanted to spit in the eye of one of them and walk out without another word but something kept me there.

They must have asked Ed Morgan to be their spokesman.

He said, 'We've talked it over, Mr Ross, and we figure we'd be no kind of help to you.'

'That's right,' said Humphress primly. 'More of a hindrance than a help.'

'Not even to help a young girl in the hands of men who'd kill their own mother if there was a dollar's profit in it?'

My question was softly put and watching them all I saw Roselaw's eyes stray over to the corner table and the two unknown riders sitting there.

'I'm sorry.' It was Ed Morgan. He spread his hands out and down in a strange movement of regret.

I reached up with my left hand and unpinned the Marshal's star on my vest. I dropped it on the floor at their feet. No one spoke. No one moved.

'When I first came here you were mighty glad to get the help of a man with a gun,' I said. 'Someone said at the time "No man rides alone" and I reckoned that maybe I'd been wrong. But not now. You'd better get yourselves another marshal.'

I turned away from them and began to make my way out when I remembered something.

I turned round and spoke to the barman.

'Where's Bear Crick?' I said.

'Bear Crick?' He had a bad habit of repeating what other men said.

'Bear Crick's what I said.'

'It's north of the Cartledge place – maybe five–six miles. Was a settlement ten years back but the folks who lived there went away.'

Once again I saw Roselaw look over at the corner table and this time something passed between him and the two riders. They made no move then and I went on out of the saloon and along the street to the little office they'd given me, thinking that maybe after all it was a bit of a laugh, the idea of Johnny Ross being a marshal. I remembered then that earlier in the evening I'd asked someone to take Bessie into the livery and feed her well. I collected my Winchester and my bedroll and was about to mosey on down to the stable when I remembered the two men in the saloon. So I cut back behind the shack and behind a few other buildings that bordered the street and I was glad I'd done so. I was just coming out from behind The Cattleman's House when I heard steps on the boardwalk. I had a peek round the corner and there were two riders and I heard one say to the other:

'We'll get him at the Pass. No use trying hyar.'

The other one grunted some kind of reply and then they swung up onto their saddles and trotted away out of town. I just picked up Bessie at the stable, bought some bacon, a tin of tomatoes and flour from a store that was still open and rode slowly in the general direction they'd taken out of Pitchfork. I hoped it was the last time but I was wrong.

CHAPTER NINE

North of the Cartledge place the bartender had said and Roselaw had given the high sign to the two hombres, in the saloon, to let 'em know I'd be on my way. And the way would be through the Pass where I'd get my comeuppance before I got too close to Bear Crick. It was pretty late now, well on towards midnight, which gave me five–six hours of darkness. I wasn't going to be able to ride round my would-be dry-gulchers in darkness and in unknown country.

I was about three miles out of Pitchfork by this time and beginning to climb up on to the benchland. I pulled in off the trail near a group of aspens. It would do for a few hours. I ground-haltered Bessie, rolled myself in my blanket and went off into a restless sleep.

I woke suddenly some time later and lay stiffly listening. Everything was still dark around me, with a fine powdering of stars high up overhead and the sound that had probably waked me came again – the distant call of a coyote. It was chilly and I shivered. I rolled out of my blanket and flapped the early autumn cold out of me. I got a small fire going and while the coffee pot heated I fed Bessie. Then I fed myself and drank hot black coffee and felt better. There were a lot of difficulties ahead of us and it was as well, I figured, to face them on a full stomach. I saddled up, kicked out the last embers of the fire, folded my bedroll and was ready. I remembered one important thing. I checked the loads in my Colt and my Winchester. Then I climbed aboard and off we went, north towards Bear Crick.

Slowly darkness lifted off the land. Pre-dawn light filtered through the trees and the first birds began to tune up ready for the big moment. It came at last, light spreading up and spilling over from the east and then fingers of gold reaching up and outwards far over to my right until at last the whole sky was ablaze.

Although they'd said that they'd wait at the Pass it was time to keep at least one eye peeled and this I did as we trotted over the wide empty plain of the benchland. A little later we came by the Cartledge ranch-house. It looked empty, dead. No smoke from the chimney. The barn gutted by the fire from which I'd saved the hosses. A length of fencing was lying flat on the ground. It was a sad desolate unhappy place.

I rode on into unknown terrain. A rough trail led down off the bench into a stretch of grazing land. The ground rose again about a mile ahead of me but the Pass was another four miles on according to the bartender. I rode on, entered a valley cutting through the hills and coming out beyond could see the high country rising up about an hour's ride ahead of me. Directly north there was a V-shaped notch in the hills and this I reckoned would be the Pass.

I arrived at a point west of the Pass and put Bessie into a canter. If this was the only way through to Bear Crick then we'd better come in sideways and unannounced. They'd count on my using the trail that led direct from Pitchfork, not knowing I'd overheard their little pow-wow outside the saloon.

Twenty minutes later and we'd reached the foot of the range. It was as I'd dimly feared. There was no way up. The cliff face rose almost sheer in front of me and this huge brown wall ran unbroken as far as I could see west of where we stood. It would probably be the same to the east at least as far as the Pass. There was nothing to do but ride east and face it out.

This took another twenty minutes over rough and rocky ground, with piles of rubble here and there where the cliff above had crumpled down into the valley. The sun was well up and beating against the cliff face and outward against us. I was beginning to work up a powerful dry. I stopped and pouring some water from my canteen I wiped Bessie's muzzle. She gave me one of her looks.

'Bessie,' I said. 'You and me. Just you and me and a mighty lot of trouble and grief ahead.'

She snorted gently and I got up into the saddle again. As I did so I saw a flash of light from way up on the hill ahead of me. There was only one explanation for that – sunlight reflecting off a gun-barrel, so I had a pretty good idea now where one of them was. The way up to the Pass must be between me and him, with his side-kick somewhere between us. The aim would be to catch me in a cross-fire. It was for me to work out just where they'd try to get me. There's always a point where two lines of fire meet. If I could assess this maybe I could ride through faster than their trigger-fingers could work and maybe I could get to Bear Crick and do something for Sarah Urquhart.

Maybe. My shirt suddenly felt cold against my back but inside something was burning me up. We hugged the last stretch of cliff face and now I could see the turn-in leading to the Pass. We reached it and I leaned forward and patted Bessie's neck.

'All right, old woman,' I said. 'Let her rip.' I tickled her not too gently with the spurs and we were away up a gentle slope, not too much for her but rising all the time. I heard the first shot then, coming from the eastern side and whining away somewhere just behind us. A second followed still coming from the east and this time overhead. I spurred Bessie on. Maybe the hombre on my side couldn't see me yet. Maybe I was too close in. There was a big cluster of house-sized rocks just a few hundred yards ahead of me. If I could hole up there I might get them separately. A third shot from over yonder skittered through the dust almost at our feet. Bessie jibbed and went up on her back legs. I fought her down. It was no time for a rodeo. We made it to the rocks in about ten seconds. I got well in among them and dismounted. We were both hot and Bessie was snorting. I pulled the Winchester out of its scabbard and edged around the rock. I peered out in the direction from which the shooting had come. At first I could see nothing but a scrub-covered hillside with more rocks dotted about it and then suddenly I spotted him. He must have figured I had gone to earth and was on his way now to get to closer quarters. It was all of three hundred yards across the wide trail between us but I brought up the rifle and took slow and steady aim. It would have to be quick or I'd have the other dry-gulcher on my back. Even then I waited another thirty seconds, until at last I had him fair and square in my sights. I gave the trigger just the right amount of slow, firm pressure and fired. At first I thought not and then I watched him reach up to his full height, stay there for a split second and then he fell forward flat on his face.

By this time I figured the other one should be reaching some vantage point. The noise of the shooting would have helped him to place me so I turned to grab Bessie's reins and realised I was too late. He was standing just above me and about thirty yards away.

He had his rifle at the ready. I didn't have a cat-in-hell's chance.

'Jest drop that gun,' he sang out, 'and stick your hands way up outa danger.'

I hesitated for a second and he put a shot about an inch away from my left boot.

'Don't try anythin', mister,' he said. 'Jest do like I said.'

I did like he said. I'm no death and glory boy. I waited while he made his way down off the narrow trail to where I was waiting.

'Lew Owens said we was to bring you in alive,' he said. 'Take your side-arm out with your right hand and jest toss it over towards me.'

I reached across and pulled my Colt from its holster and threw it towards him. He waited, taking no chance at all. Then he dismounted by bringing his left leg round over the saddle-horn and jumping lightly to the ground.

'Reckon you musta drilled Pete or he'd've showed up by now.'

He came a little closer. I noticed he'd got

his lariat in his left hand.

'We'll have to tie you up,' he said. 'Turn round, mister, and go on grabbin' the air.'

I turned and something that felt like a ton of bricks but was probably the barrel of a gun smacked into the back of my skull. The ground reared up towards me and I seemed to be falling a long, long way through darkness.

When I came to I still seemed to be looking into darkness but there was light round the edges. There was a strong smell of earth in my nostrils and then I knew I was lying face down with my hands tied together under me. I must have moved for a shadow moved somewhere close at hand and a voice I was getting to dislike said: 'Glad you ain't daid. Lew Owens wouldn't have liked that. He aims to kill you daid hisself.'

I felt his hands grab my shoulders and heave me up and round until I was in a sitting position. I was near blinded by the light and my head throbbed. I sure felt sorry for Johnny Ross.

'Git up,' said my captor. 'It's time to mosey on outa hyar.'

I got up and he bundled me up on to Bessie's back.

'I'll be jest behind you, mister. So ride on and don't try any monkey tricks.'

I realised then that he had tied my hands with his lariat and that he had the other end, either in his hand or tied to his saddle-horn.

'Git goin',' he said. 'We've got a coupla hours in the saddle before you see yore old pal, Lew.'

It was then I started to plan my escape. The rope linking us would be pretty taut most of the time. It couldn't well be otherwise. I had to wait for a chance of pulling him clean out of his saddle and of getting to him before he could get to his gun. It wasn't much of a plan but I couldn't think of a better one on the spur of the moment. He'd said a coupla hours so I had plenty of time to select the right moment, the right place. We had now moved on up the trail to the Pass and the hills were beginning to shoulder in on us. It was about time for a little chat, I reckoned.

'You got a name?' I sung out.

'What's that to you?' he growled.

'Nothin',' I said. 'Still, it's mighty nice if the condemned man knows the name of the hangman.'

'Nothin' I'd like better than to have the hanging of the likes of you,' he said. 'But you're Lew Owens' game, mister. He's the one who's a-goin' to have the fun.' And then, as if remembering my question he said, 'I'm Sam Backus. Maybe that'll make you think twice afore you try any tricks.'

I remembered the name from way down the trail. An unimportant member of the Ringo gang down in Arizona. He'd once shot a town-marshal in the back and had lived on it ever since.

'Sam Backus,' I said. 'Sam Backus. Yeah, the name's kinda familiar. Ain't you the hombre that stole a little girl's savings down in Arizona? Or are you the one that's been running so long, you don't know whether

187

you're a'comin' or a'goin'?'

His answer to this was a string of bad words followed by a tug on the lariat to show me who was master.

'Keep movin' an' shut yore trap,' he ended, 'or I'll shut it for you once and for all.'

We'd reached level ground now. Fairly high up, with plenty of piñon and scrub-oak scattered about and what looked like the real high country in the distance, with great peaks rising up into the blue bowl of the sky and snow gleaming white on their sides. It was what I'd come a long way to see but hadn't figured I'd see it as I was now. In a short time we'd be going downgrade and I could see ahead that from then on we'd be climbing steadily again. It would be a lot easier to unseat him as we went down so it would have to be soon.

We rode on for another five or more minutes. It was hot on the side of the hills and I could feel sweat running down my neck. The trail suddenly steepened and I reckoned the moment had come. I wanted him to tighten up the rope again.

'What are you aimin' to do when this little party's over, Sam? Shoot a few more gents in the back or start stealin' milk bottles from babies?'

'You goddam sonofabitch,' he yelled and at once pulled the rope taut. This was it. I gave a dry-throated imitation of a rebel yell and at the same second yanked my tied wrists out and forward. Bessie helped by trying to climb up into the sky and the next thing I knew I was falling backwards. I landed on something soft, a body. I twisted desperately as he yelled out in pain and chopped my two pinioned hands hard down on the back of his neck. He gave out a sort of strangled grunt and went limp and soft. I got my knees astride him in case he came awake and started to work on the rope. It took longer than I'd expected but at last I got the knots untied and was free.

Sam Backus had to be got rid of. That was for sure. He was still sleeping quiet and peaceful so I took his boots off and stuffed them into my saddle-bag. Then I took his Colt out of its holster and flung it as far as I could among some rocks. Even if he found it it probably wouldn't be much good to him. I stripped his gunbelt of ammunition and then I turned to Bessie and got her ready for the last stage of the journey to Bear Crick. By the time I'd wiped her down and fed her some oats, Sam Backus was beginning to stir and twitch. I drew my gun and waited. Very slowly he came to his senses, his eyes opening and staring up into the sky. Then he slowly heaved himself into a sitting position and stared at me as if he didn't quite believe what he was seeing.

'Time to be on your way, Sam,' I said.

'Way? Which way?' He sure looked mighty puzzled.'

'The way to Pitchfork and make it snappy. My trigger-finger's beginning to itch.'

He looked at his feet then. 'On foot?' he said. 'I cain't git to Pitchfork without my boots.'

'You sure can and sure will. If I see you

again, Sam Backus, in two minutes from now, I'll shoot you down. Git goin'.'

I waggled the barrel of my gun a little and this brought him to his feet.

'If you take it nice an' slow,' I said, 'you'll get to town by mornin'.'

'My God, mister, ain't you got any pity?'

'Nope,' I said. 'None at all. Leastwise, not for skunks like you. On your way.'

He stared at me, for a few moments and then turned and marched off up the Pass heading south. I watched him out of sight and then I climbed up on to Bessie's patient old back and rode on towards whatever kind of hell was waiting for me in the place called Bear Crick.

CHAPTER TEN

As we clip-clopped along the winding trail that fell and then began to rise again fairly sharply I reckoned on maybe a couple of hours' riding. I'd figure out what to do when I got there. No good planning ahead when you haven't one little idea of the place or the folks in it.

It was now well on into the afternoon and I came to a good broad yellow meadow lying like a carpet on the side of the green pine-covered hills. On the far side there were more trees, high ponderosas and through them the trail led, dim but clear enough for me. We jogged on for what seemed a long time, came out on the far side of the forest and crossed another wide tawny-yellow meadow. Far over the sun dipped down behind the big hills and a steady golden light spread like a vast curtain across the sky. It was a time for a man to be at ease, at peace, but instead here I was urging old Bessie on and driven inside by a powerful kind of anxiety.

At the far side of the meadow we came to a sudden halt. The ground fell away below me, deep down, into a wide canyon. Along it ran a narrow golden ribbon of water and far over on the other side and about a mile from where I was I could make out a small huddle of houses where the canyon wall folded back. I was looking down at Bear Crick. The little settlement was the hole-in-the-wall, the robbers' roost I'd come a long way to find. Lew Owens and his pals were holed up here and in one of the houses Sarah Urquhart was waiting for me.

I angled Bessie along the canyon rim until we reached a place where we could ride down. We slithered and slid a good bit of the way but made it at last just as the blue twilight flowed in around us. It would soon be dark. I didn't reckon it would be much good riding up to the settlement in daylight and getting shot down before I even knocked on a door. I waited at the foot of the hill down which I'd come until it was almost full dark. Then I rode to the creek, forded it and rode leisurely towards the settlement. Yellow light splashed out from a window not far ahead. Up in the trees to my right an owl hooted. I pulled in under some tall pines about a hundred yards from the first building. I tied Bessie to a branch. Then I checked the loads in my Colt. Everything was fine. All I had to do was walk in, shoot down five–six hombres and walk out again with Sarah Urquhart under my arm. I shivered and up in the trees the owl cried again. It was dark now except for the lamplight in the window. Keeping to the cover of the trees I moved on towards the dark huddle of buildings. Suddenly a door opened in a side wall and light spilled out into the darkness. I froze. A man slung the contents of a bucket out into the night. He paused for a couple of seconds, seeming to look up at the first stars. Then he turned and went in slamming the door behind him. I let out a long slow breath and moved quietly on. I wanted a look in through that lighted window before I decided on a plan of action. I got within about ten feet of the nearest building and a man laughed high and shrill from somewhere within. I waited in a heart-throbbing silence but nothing happened. I got up under the lee of the building and moved slowly towards the open window.

I could just about hear the murmur of voices and then again the same man laughed. I was now only a couple of inches from the window. I moved again and poked my left eye round the frame. I was looking into a fairly long room with a home-made bar consisting of planks laid lengthwise on four barrels. It was some kind of a saloon. Standing against the bar there were three men. Two I knew. One was Sam Point, the other was Jake Gillams. I'd met them at the Cartledge place. The third man was short and square-set. I didn't know him. There was no sign of Lew Owens. I could hear them now quite clearly.

Jake Gillams said, 'Now she's signed, what's the next move?'

'Rests with Lew, I reckon,' said Point. 'He did all the persuadin' an' most of the thinkin'.'

'We'll have to get rid of her,' said the short square-set man. 'She'll be a danger 'long as she's alive.'

'You gotta point there, friend,' said Point. 'Mebbe Lew has that in mind. Anyways we'll know when he's had his beauty sleep.'

I got the picture all right. Sarah Urquhart must have signed over the cattle and maybe the ranch. I preferred not to think how she'd been made to do that. But what mattered now was to get her away before they killed her. I couldn't count on Lew Owens remaining asleep all night. It would have to be now. I cast around desperately for a plan. If I bust into the room I might get one of them: maybe two. But the third would get me and there was still Lew Owens and maybe three-four more of the gang really to crack down on Johnny Ross. Well, there was only one good way I figured and that was the old fire trick. Set fire to a building and do your shooting when folks come a-running out as they most always do, not wanting to be burned up inside a building. The first problem was getting a real fire going. For this I needed more than just a match. I'd have to find the stable if there was one and use straw.

I back-tracked away from the window, got to the corner of the building and looked around. Beyond it I could see another barn-like shack, with a large dark opening in its front. It could be a stable. I moved out from the shelter of the house and across the open space between it and the second building. I got to the big open door and waited. Somewhere inside there was a rustling movement and a slight snorting noise. I'd struck lucky first time. The gang's mounts all tucked up for a quiet night.

I snuck in and found a lantern hanging on a nail just inside the door. I'd need this too. I moved farther in and found hay stacked up against a side wall. This would all need time. Then it struck me that I was all kinds of a damn fool. The fire would do just as well here. The gang would come a-running if they thought their hosses were in danger. My first job was to get the broncs out. I edged in, listening as I did so. There were five of them. I had to get them untied, start them on their way out and get the fire going before someone raised the alarm. I started with the one farthest into the barn. He snorted a bit and fancy-danced around but I soon had him loose. Then I got to work on the others until all five of them were free. It was getting tricky now working away in the dark with five broncs moving around and getting more and more scairt of the goings-on. I grabbed a pile of hay and heaped it up between the door and the wooden side of the barn. Then I opened the lantern and poured kerosene all over the pile. I added another big armful of hay for good measure. Then I went around behind the horses and gave one loud yell. They whinnied with fear and one of them started pawing the air.

Then suddenly they were off through the door.

I lit a match and dropped it on the hay. For a moment nothing happened. Then the flame reached the kerosene and up it went in a fine golden-red blaze of light. It was time to go. I ran out fast and made for the shelter of the trees just opposite the saloon. The noise of the hosses stampeding out into the night must have reached them. A door was flung open and out they came, Sam Point, Jake Gillams, the short man and a fourth jigger wearing an apron.

'What the hell!' one of them shouted. Flame had suddenly shot up the side of the barn.

I waited for a little more light and, waiting, knew I couldn't shoot them down from ambush. That was their way. Maybe once it would have been mine. But I'd worn a star, if only for a few days.

I walked out from the trees with my Colt in my left hand.

'All right,' I yelled. 'Shuck your guns,

gents. The game's over.'

They all stared at my half-seen figure. Light increased as the barn began to burn up.

'Jump him!' one of them shouted. 'He's alone.'

One of them fell flat. Two others jumped to the side reaching for their guns as they did so. I triggered off a shot at the one on the right and he spun round with a scream. Two guns roared. A slug whistled past my shoulder. A second whiplashed the dust at my feet. I halted, took good aim at the man on the left. He fired again and missed again. I fired and he reached up on his toes, his hands came out clawing and then he too slumped to the ground. The man on the ground started up and ran towards the door.

I yelled at him and he turned in a quick desperate movement firing from low down. My Colt roared again and he fell, grabbing at his leg. I began to move towards him. He stuck a hand up in the air. The other was holding on to his leg.

'All right. All right,' he cried. 'I give in.'

His gun was lying on the step near him. I picked it up and pitched it out into the darkness.

I bent down and grabbed him by his shirt. 'Where's Lew Owens?' I said. 'I want him.'

His face stared up at me pale and scared.

'He's sleepin', mister. In the room upstairs.'

'Not now, he isn't,' I said. 'Not after all this hullabaloo.'

I let him go. Somewhere inside were Lew Owens and Sarah Urquhart. I went into the long, empty bar-room. The only light came from a kerosene lamp on a shelf behind the home-made bar. I stood dead still, listening. There was someone else in the room and there was only one place he could be.

'All right,' I said. 'Come out, slow and careful.'

A head appeared above the level of the bar-top. It was round as a harvest moon and decorated with long drooping moustaches. It was the hombre who'd sported an apron.

'Who're you?' I snapped at him.

'I just cook an' clean, mister. Just cook an' clean. All this means nothing to me. Nothing a-tall.'

He was so all-fired anxious to please that he was repeating himself.

'Where's Lew Owens?' I said.

'He'll be upstairs, mister, in bed.'

'Reckon not. Not now. How many rooms up there?'

'Three,' he said.

'Which one's the girl in?'

'The girl?'

'Goddam you. The girl,' I said. 'Miss Urquhart. The one you and your pals kidnapped.'

'Not me, mister. Not me. I jest cook an' clean.'

He was like a parrot I'd once heard in a bar in San Antone. I waggled the end of the Colt at him.

'Quick,' I said. 'Or I'll blow your head off.'

'She's tied up, mister, in the room off the one Lew Owens is in.'

'Right,' I said and made for the door

beyond the bar. It opened into a dark staircase and I went up on the balls of my feet ready for anything to explode. It didn't. There was a kind of landing at the top. Two doors led off it. I chose the farthest away from me. I kicked it in and found myself in a bedroom with a brass bedstead and nothing else. There was a second door across the room. I yelled out, 'I'm waiting, Lew Owens.'

No one answered but I heard a faint noise that might or might not be a window opening. There was just no sense in waiting so I kicked this second door in and waited again with my gun cocked and ready. Still no sound. Then something fell with a crash outside the house. I pounded into the room and could just make out the shape of a window. I crossed and looked out and a voice floated up out of the darkness.

'Can't wait now, Johnny. See you in Pitchfork and we'll settle the account.'

It was Lew Owens and before I could even close my mouth, he was off into the darkness on the one horse that hadn't been in the stable. He must have had it hidden behind the saloon ready for some such moment as this.

'Aha!' said a small voice behind me. 'If it isn't Sir Galahad in person.'

I stuck my gun back in its holster.

'Don't know nothin' about any Sir Gallyhead,' I said. 'I've just come to take you home.'

'I'm all tied up like a chicken,' she said in a small, tired sort of way. 'Could you untie me, Johnny?'

'It'll be easier down in the bar-room with a light,' I said. 'Where are you?'

'In the corner.'

I found her and reaching down managed to pick her up in my arms. She was no featherweight but somehow or other I got her through the room, along the landing and down the stairs. Then in the bar-room I saw her for the first time that night. Her hair was a mess, her pants and shirt all mussed-up and down her dirty face tears were running.

'Look,' I said, kind of stern. 'This ain't the

time for hysterics. Just let me get these ropes off.'

'Yes,' she said, but her eyes contained a glint that I'd seen before. Well, I got the main knots undone and was just releasing her when there was a clumping of boots on the porch outside and then the door sprang open.

I reached for my gun and my groping hand suddenly stopped. The first man in was a tall bearded homesteader I'd met at the Cartledge place. It was Joshua Brill and behind him came two more like him. They were all carrying long, old-fashioned rifles. Two more men came in carrying the man I'd shot through the leg. They dropped him on to the floor in a corner.

'There's two dead men outside,' said one of the homesteaders.

'Yes,' I said, slowly letting out a breath I'd been holding for some time. 'Yes, I killed 'em.'

'We heard that Point and the others had kidnapped the Urquhart girl,' said Brill

206

awkwardly. 'We've had troubles with the Urquharts but we don't make war on women. We came over to set things right.'

I stood up and Sarah Urquhart got to her feet too. The barman, cleaner and cook was still standing where I'd left him. I said, 'If you want to get off lightly, you'd better rustle up some grub and a few gallons of coffee.'

He said, 'Yes, sir,' and disappeared into a cubby-hole behind the bar.

Two of the homesteaders tended to the wounded man's leg and then we tucked into the food the cook had prepared.

'Where are my cattle now, Mr Brill?' said Sarah Urquhart.

'They're all bedded down out on the flats west of the canyon,' said Brill. 'Tomorrow we'll drive 'em back to your place.'

'Why did you do it, Mr Brill?' she asked.

He gave her a steady honest-sort-of-look.

'When they first came here we thought they were like us, that they'd help us keep what we'd worked for, that they were our kind. After the killing of Ep Cartledge we were pretty mad, but when they said we should drive off the Urquhart cattle we agreed. It was only after we'd stopped to think a bit that we knew we'd done wrong. It kinda hit us then that they weren't our kind after all. They were the other kind, outlaws, beasts of prey. They've only got what they deserved.'

Well, after a little more humble-pie and explanation the apple-knockers trailed off with their long rifles. Someone put the wounded man in bed and Miss Sarah Urquhart and I were left looking kind of warily at each other by the bar.

'Well,' I said. 'That's that, as they say.'

'They?' she said. 'Who are "they"?'

'Folks,' I said. 'Just folks like you and me.'

I sure had worked up a powerful interest in this girl but it didn't look as if it would come to much, seeing that every time we got together we bickered like a couple of fighting cocks.

'What happens now?' she said.

'Come first light and I'm dragging it to Pitchfork,' I said.

'Why?'

'There's a small matter I have to settle with a gent called Lew Owens,' I said.

A shadow of some strange emotion moved on her face. I wondered whether it was fear.

'You don't have to settle with Lew Owens on my account,' she said.

'It's nothing to do with your account,' I said. 'This matter goes back to a time before I met you.'

'Oh!' she said, her frosty eyes shining with curiosity.

'Yep,' I said. 'To the bad old days when I rode the outlaw trail. Remind me to tell you all about it some day.'

'I won't forget,' she said, with something approaching a smile.

'And now you promise me you'll leave well alone and stay away from Lew Owens and Pitchfork.'

'Nope,' I said, pretty firm.

'Not even for my sake?' she said, softly.

'Nope,' I said, looking firmly in the other direction. 'Not even for you, ma'am.'

'Oh, well,' she said, after a short and thoughtful pause. 'Then I'd better come along too and keep an eye on you.'

There was nothing I could say but I decided I'd get away before first light and get my business done before she could start horning in on my affairs.

She said, 'I'll get some sleep in the room upstairs. Give me a shout when you're ready to go and I'll be with you.' She turned away and marched over to the door that led upstairs. 'Good night, Johnny Ross,' she called out and was gone.

CHAPTER ELEVEN

I had bedded down in a blanket and my head on my saddle in the bar-room, somewhere about midnight, I guess. I seemed to wake up about five minutes later. I groped around for my watch and a match, and found it was a half after five and close to first light. Now was the time I figured to outsmart Miss Urquhart. I tiptoed round in my stockinged feet and got a small fire going and a coffee pot boiling. I found some cold bacon and some hard biscuit and before you could say 'Jiminy' I was comfortably tucking away grub and lapping hot coffee. I had just finished the bacon and had the mug of coffee half-way to my mouth when I heard the faint creak of wood – from the direction of the staircase. Some mighty rude words came to my lips but they weren't any use.

Before I could even put the mug down on the bar-top there she was as large as life, smiling at me from the doorway, as pretty as a picture on a tomato can.

'Well,' she said, 'here we are bright and early and all ready for the big day in Pitchfork.'

She hopped over to the coffee pot and peeked in just like a nosy bird.

'You mind if I help myself to some of this brew?' she said.

'Yep,' I said, not being overly fond of bright converse at the beginning of the day. I should have said 'Nope' but was a bit confused. She helped herself and nibbled some biscuit.

'I'm ready whenever you are,' she said, sweetly.

And that's how the last part of the story began with me and Sarah Urquhart riding away from the little settlement of Bear Crick, empty now of everyone, except the wounded man and the barman to look after him and the dead outlaws waiting in cold and sullen silence for their last resting-place to be dug.

We rode for a pretty long time in silence, back up on to the benchland, over the wide meadows and through the tall timber. It was only when we got to the Pass that I made another effort to dissuade her from coming any farther.

'There's no kind of sense in you coming to Pitchfork, Miss Urquhart,' I said.

'There's every kind of sense, Mr Ross. First I aim to keep an eye on you and second I reckon I'd better do something about that bill of sale that those men made me sign.'

'It'll be Lew Owens who has that,' I said.

'The one with the cruel smile,' she said.

'You might call it a smile,' I said. 'It's more of a twist of the mouth, to my way of thinking.'

'You said you met him down the trail.'

'Yes, I met him down in Arizona territory. That's how I came by this.' I held up my busted right hand.

213

'Ah yes,' she said gravely. 'Your poor hand. I had wondered about it.'

'It's not a very pretty story,' I said. 'And all that matters now is – that we settle things once and for all.'

We went on quietly for a time down the south side of the Pass and out into the barren stretch leading to the hills. There was still one question scratching away in my head like a mouse trying to get out.

'About that bill of sale,' I said. 'What's on it?'

'That I've sold the cattle for five dollars cash down,' she said.

'That wouldn't hold up in any court of law,' I said.

'I signed it.'

'You signed it?'

'I had to,' she said.

I looked across at her. She looked ahead of her, far ahead.

'Did they mistreat you?'

'Yes,' she said quietly. 'Yes. They mistreated me.'

She said no more, just stared ahead of her. I felt like someone had placed a cold hand on my heart. There was nothing I could say but I rode on and an anger I had never known before rode with me.

We covered the rest of the distance in a couple of hours. Just at the edge of town she pulled in.

'It's not too late to stop now,' she said. 'I don't want any more bloodshed, any more killing. There's enough already on the conscience of the Urquharts.'

I said, 'This has nothin' to do with you, Miss Urquhart. I aim to settle with Lew Owens and that's all.' I looked at her squarely. There was something I had to say and it took a lot of courage to say it.

'Just a few paces down this street,' I said, 'there's a shack on which you will see the words, "Marshal's Office". It was mine for a few days and I figure no one will object if I use it again for a short space. I want for you to go there and wait for me. When I've finished my business I'll be back and I'll

215

have a few words to say to you.'

'Yes,' she said. 'I see.'

We rode on a bit farther and reined in outside the shack. She dismounted and led the horse to the tie-rail. Then she stood in the doorway and said, 'I'll be waiting.'

I tipped my hat and rode away in the direction of the saloon. It was almost noon, with the sun high and not a soul to be seen. It was a dusty sun-dried place waiting for the first rains. I reined in again outside the saloon and tied Bessie to the rail. I figured that, if Lew Owens was anywhere, it would be here, in The Cattleman's House, Rose-law's place, and I knew pretty well which side Roselaw was on.

I walked up the steps and turned before going in. A window drape across the street in Ed Morgan's store slipped back into place. Pitchfork was always watching, an uneasy town, with no kind of pride. I shrugged and pushed the bat-wings inward. It was dark inside but I was ready if Lew Owens was there. Roselaw was behind the bar. His

216

mouth was open with surprise, shock or maybe fear.

I said, 'Howdy, Mr Roselaw. You look kinda surprised to see me.'

He just stood there gulping and speechless.

'I'll have a drink,' I said. 'For old times' sake.'

He got a bottle off the shelf behind him and pushed it unsteadily towards me.

'I'll have a glass too,' I said.

The glass followed the bottle over the polished bar-top. I stood up close to it and poured myself a drink and drank it down. There was no one else there.

'You know why I'm here,' I said.

He nodded, still short on words. Sweat was beginning to gather on his forehead and upper lip.

'They … they forced my hand, Mr Ross. They made me do it. Said they'd kill me if I didn't work in with them.'

'Who killed Ed Urquhart, Roselaw?'

His face went white with fear. He turned and stared at the door beyond the bar. A single sweat drop fell from his chin on to the bar.

'I don't know, Mr Ross,' he muttered. 'Honest, I don't know.'

'Why don't you tell him, Roselaw?' said a mocking voice from the far end of the room, almost exactly behind me. 'Why don't you tell Mr Ross that I killed Ed Urquhart?'

I whirled, dragging at my Colt. I was too late, as always. A gun exploded before I'd even cleared leather. A slug smashed into the mirror behind me smashing it to bits. I could see Owens and I fired but missed. His gun boomed again, light blooming out of the muzzle. He'd missed a second time and I ran round the far corner of the bar and waited. I needed a moment's breathing space bad.

'Come out, Johnny Ross,' he taunted. 'You can only die once. Come on out, you yellow-bellied little skunk.'

I said, 'Lew Owens, I give you five seconds in which to hand over that paper you made Miss Urquhart sign and then surrender. I'll take you in and see you get a fair trial. If you don't throw in your hand in five seconds I'll come and get you.'

I didn't bother to count aloud but I gave him a good five seconds and then I came out from behind the bar. For a second there was nothing and then a gun exploded from way over to the left of where he'd been, once, twice, three times. Something plucked at my coat sleeve and my gun bucked once and again hard against the palm of my left hand. He suddenly seemed to stand up fair and square and right in front of me and my third bullet took him full in the chest. His legs buckled and he crumpled down on to the floor. I walked over and looked down at him. It wasn't only Lew Owens I had killed. I was killing the past, I guess, leaving it behind once and for all, dead as the outlaw who now lay stretched out on the bar-room floor before me.

Slowly I holstered my gun and turned towards the doors of the saloon. Then I remembered something and I went back to the body of Lew Owens. I knelt down by him and felt in the inner pocket of his vest. It was there as I'd guessed. A folded sheet of cheap paper. It had Sarah Urquhart's signature on it. I stuck it away in one of my pockets and stood up and started to walk out. A voice behind me said, 'All this was none of my doing,' but I went on, not wanting to have any more truck with Roselaw or anyone else in the fair town of Pitchfork.

I untied Bessie and walked her towards the place where I'd left Sarah Urquhart. She was waiting for me and already in the saddle. She watched me with a strange attentiveness as I drew near her.

'I guess there's only one place left to go to,' she said.

I said, 'Yes,' and swung up into the saddle and away we rode out of the town and along the trail to the Urquhart ranch.

When we got there she climbed out of the saddle and when I'd climbed down too she stood by me, silently, looking at the deserted ranch-house, the empty corrals and the tawny-yellow rangeland beyond.

'Look, Johnny Ross,' she said at last. 'What you need is someone to look after you, someone to stop you ramboodling all over the place and generally raising hell.'

She sure was the most outspokenest girl I'd ever met.

'If you mean what I think you mean,' I said, 'then you ought to know I'm not the marrying kind.'

'I am,' she said.

'Now look here, Miss Urquhart,' I said. 'This is all wrong. Women don't propose to men – leastwise, not in my book, they don't.'

'That's the trouble with you, Johnny Ross,' she said. 'You've got all your ideas on what's right and what's wrong out of some goldarned book. Life's quite different from what they say about it in books.' She paused, then said, 'Look at me, Johnny Ross.'

I looked. I had to. And by Jiminy there was something in her eyes I'd never seen before. They said something I could hardly believe about Sarah Urquhart and Johnny Ross and

221

hearing it I knew life would never be quite the same again. So I took her in my arms and 'Yes,' I said. 'Yes.'